Amina

TITLES IN THIS SERIES

Shahana (Kashmir)

Amina (Somalia)

Naveed (Afghanistan)

Emilio (Mexico)

Malini (Sri Lanka)

Zafir (Syria)

THROUGH MY EYES

series editor Lyn White

Amina

J.L. POWERS

ALLEN&UNWIN

SYDNEY·MELBOURNE·AUCKLAND·LONDON

Australian Government

This project has been assisted by the Australian Government through the Australia Council for the Arts, its arts funding and advisory body.

A portion of the proceeds (up to $5000) from sales of this series will be donated to UNICEF. UNICEF works in over 190 countries, including those in which books in this series are set, to promote and protect the rights of children. www.unicef.org.au

First published in 2013

Allen & Unwin
83 Alexander Street, Crows Nest NSW 2065, Australia
Phone: (61 2) 8425 0100
Email: info@allenandunwin.com
Web: www.allenandunwin.com

A Cataloguing-in-Publication entry is available from
the National Library of Australia – www.trove.nla.gov.au

ISBN 978 174331 249 0

Teaching and learning guide available from www.allenandunwin.com

Cover and text design by Bruno Herfst & Vincent Agostino
Set in 11pt Plantin
Cover photos: Mogadishu street © African Union – United Nations Mission in Darfur (UNAMID), portrait of a young girl © Ariadne Van Zandbergen/Getty Images 2012. Every effort has been made to trace the original source of copyright images contained in this book. The publishers would be pleased to hear from copyright holders of any errors or omissions.
Map of Somalia by Guy Holt
This book was printed in March 2015 at Griffin Press,
168 Cross Keys Road, Salisbury South, SA 5106

10 9 8 7 6 5

The paper in this book is FSC® certified.
FSC® promotes environmentally responsible, socially beneficial and economically viable management of the world's forests.

For the gracious Somalis
I met on my journey
writing this book
and for children growing up
in conflict zones
in all parts of the world.

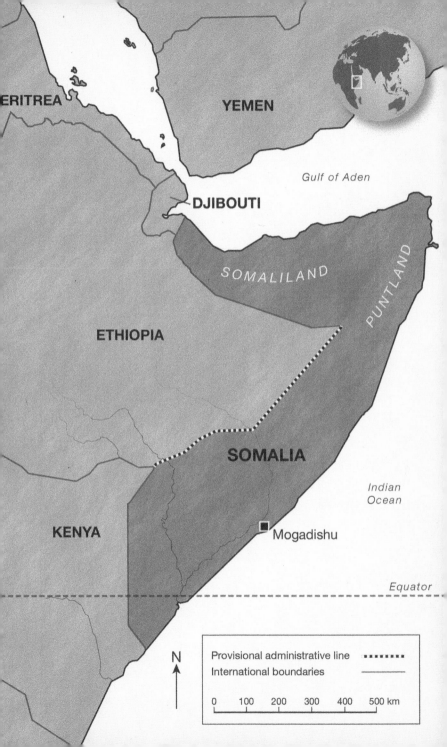

ERITREA

YEMEN

Gulf of Aden

DJIBOUTI

SOMALILAND

PUNTLAND

ETHIOPIA

SOMALIA

*Indian
Ocean*

KENYA

■ Mogadishu

Equator

N

Provisional administrative line ▪▪▪▪▪▪
International boundaries ──────

0   100   200   300   400   500 km

Chapter 1

Amina inched down the broken concrete steps and skirted the rubble in her yard as she walked from the house to her father's studio. She knocked gently.

'Aabbe,' she whispered. 'Aabbe.'

He opened the door. Even though he was frowning, Amina laughed at the streak of green paint smeared across his cheek and his blue lips. He sometimes sucked a paintbrush while deep in thought.

'Sorry to disturb you, Aabbe,' she said. 'Hooyo says you've been working too long and need to eat something.'

It was true, Aabbe had been in his studio since last night after Maghrib prayers. He kept a sijaayad rolled up under his table, which he unfurled and kneeled upon for prayers whenever he didn't go to mosque. No matter how hard he worked, he always prayed five times a day, like a devout Muslim should.

Aabbe glanced at his paintbrush. He looked lost.

Amina put her hand on her father's shoulder, knowing

that sometimes human touch was all he needed to come back to the real world.

It worked instantly. Light returned to his eyes. 'Amina,' he said.

'Can I see your painting?'

'Yes. Yes, of course.' He stepped aside and Amina ducked her head to pass through the low doorway.

A clutter of art materials and blank canvases lay scattered in piles all around the room. These days, the materials were too expensive for Aabbe to share with Amina the way he sometimes used to, back when the two of them would paint together. He still let her use black and white acrylics and charcoal, but she had given up colour and canvases.

Now Amina was no longer sure what she would paint if her father presented her with a perfectly blank, white canvas. She had learned to use the ruins of her city to create art. She drew pictures and wrote poems on the fragments of walls left standing after bomb and grenade attacks; she hoarded strips of cloth, broken glass and the wreckage of buildings for other projects she planned in secret at home. The debris *was* her canvas, the detritus of war her personal collection of art materials. And the itch in her fingertips drove her to keep creating, no matter how dangerous it was to do it.

'Ohhhhhh.' Amina sucked in her breath when she saw her father's latest painting, an unfurling of grey-green, white-capped waves rolling far from shore. Only the ocean and the sky. No land, no boats, no people – not his usual paintings of Mogadishu's bombed-out buildings and abandoned streets, displaced people squatting with their goats in the city's ruins, or grim battle scenes. It was so realistic, it looked like a photograph.

'You were inspired,' she said. 'It's *beautiful*.'

'Yes, Allah willed it,' he agreed. 'But its beauty is an illusion. An entire world exists underneath the ocean's surface – a world of life and death and blood. Predators killing those who are weaker and smaller.'

Amina thought about all that lay below the waves. Sharks and whales and jellyfish. All the things that hunted and stung and devoured other fish.

Of course, even though it looked like a simple ocean scene, to Aabbe it meant much more. He always had a deeper meaning in mind; he always intended his paintings to comment on life in Somalia. For this reason, a painting by Samatar Khalid was dangerous and sold only on the black market. From there, it made its way to the far-flung corners of the world, wherever the Somali diaspora had found a home.

'Let's go,' Aabbe said. 'Your mother is waiting.'

He fumbled underneath a cabinet, knocking down a roll of drawings as he retrieved his slippers. He sighed, then held the door open for Amina.

Amina squinted at the hot sun as a large black stork took flight from the wall surrounding the house, one claw scrabbling against the bright blue shards of glass cemented to the top to keep people from climbing over.

She shivered, hoping the bird wasn't a sign of death.

Amina had never known her city without war. Somalia had descended into civil war several years before she was born. Though there had been many attempts to create a stable, strong government, none had succeeded. Instead, the city's neighbourhoods had become war strips between rival war lords. A few years ago, a group of Islamic courts had united to oppose the government and wrest power from the war lords. Then, with the support of Ethiopian and African Union soldiers – a coalition of soldiers from other African nations who were backed by the United Nations – the government returned to power and the Islamic Courts Union fled the city. For a very short time, it had seemed as though Mogadishu might have finally found peace. Instead, a militant group calling itself al-Shabaab splintered off from the Islamic Courts Union and started fighting the government.

The war lords had been gangsters, Aabbe liked to say. But al-Shabaab soldiers were worse because they pretended that Allah blessed their criminal activities.

Since then, al-Shabaab had taken control of most of the city's neighbourhoods while the government stockaded itself in Villa Somalia, the presidential palace. Recently, some of the men from the Islamic Courts Union had joined with the government; together, they were battling al-Shabaab with the help of African Union soldiers.

It gave Amina a headache just to think about it. The names and identities of the groups battling on Mogadishu's streets were constantly shifting. Only one thing remained certain: the world she lived in was a dangerous and unpredictable place.

Last year, during a four-day skirmish between al-Shabaab and government soldiers, somebody had launched a grenade right onto the roof of their house. The second storey had caved in, collapsing the roof and one of the walls. Their living room had been destroyed along with Amina's and her older brother Roble's bedrooms. The lower level was still intact and that was where the family now lived. Now, Roble slept in the front room, which doubled as their living room, and Amina shared a bedroom with her grandmother, Ayeeyo. Then there was Aabbe and Hooyo's room, the kitchen, the bathroom and the toilet.

Roble had worked with Aabbe to prop up the kitchen ceiling with beams so that it didn't disintegrate from the weight of the rubble above it. Still, Amina couldn't work in the kitchen without worrying that, suddenly and without warning, she would get buried alive.

Even if it was dangerous, she still liked to climb the stairs next to the kitchen at the back of the house to the second storey. An entire wall had toppled over into the yard below, leaving an open space on the top floor where Amina could see the world.

Up there, she liked to watch the ocean. The sun glared back at her from ripples and gentle waves. She sometimes heard the gentle buzzing of drones as they passed overhead, the sounds of BBC Somalia broadcast on a radio at a nearby cafe and the discord of different imams calling the men to prayer, their voices broadcast from loudspeakers at each mosque. She'd watch as men went in twos and threes to the mosques, as soldiers patrolled the streets, as boys kicked a soccer ball a few blocks away.

Aabbe and Amina walked up the steps and into the house.

◆▬◆

'Hooyo!' Amina called to her mother from the front room. 'Aabbe is here!'

Amina's mother shuffled out of the kitchen. 'Samatar!' Her hand rested on her belly, just now beginning to bulge though she was already almost six months with child. 'I set aside soor with lots of butter, just the way you like it.'

They usually ate maraq with the corn meal but vegetables and meat had become both scarce and expensive due to the drought afflicting the entire region. Saliva gathered in Amina's mouth just thinking of the salty stew with meat and tomatoes, served over rice. Her mother used to make the dish when they had more money – fresh banana on the side, of course. They ate bananas with everything. Roble joked that it wasn't a meal without bananas.

Aabbe sat on a mat near the front window and Amina brought water and a towel. She knelt beside him, placing a bowl in front of him. He splashed water on his face and rubbed his hands dry with the towel she handed him, then poured water over his hands, rubbing them vigorously to make them clean.

Hooyo brought a dish piled high with thick soor and sliced banana. Aabbe ate with his right hand, butter dripping off his fingers and running down his elbow. When he was finished, Amina brought the water again and he washed his hands.

Hooyo sat in a chair nearby and the two of them spoke in quiet voices. Amina liked the way they looked at each other, as though they were still young and in love. But she quickly grew bored of their conversation, and she didn't even realise she was kicking the wall with her heel until Hooyo looked over sharply and said, 'Stop it, Amina. The bombs have done enough damage to our house without you kicking a wall down also.'

Amina shared a secret, guilty smile with her father. Hooyo was always after her to act more like a young woman, but Amina still felt like a little girl. She missed being able to run and play. She missed the easy relationships with her male cousins, suddenly strained, even though she had grown up with them and they were like brothers. Now she had to cover her head and arms, showing only her face, whenever she was around any man besides her father and brother.

Aabbe and Hooyo returned to their conversation. Whatever they were discussing so intently, it seemed important.

When Roble came inside, sweaty from playing soccer, Aabbe and Hooyo glanced up.

'How was the game?' Hooyo asked.

Roble grinned. 'I scored a goal.'

'It is a big risk you take, son,' Hooyo said.

Al-Shabaab had outlawed soccer. One of Aabbe's colleagues at the university had been arrested and thrown into jail just for *talking* about soccer! They claimed soccer kept people from prayer – though Amina had seen all the boys pause in the middle of a game and go to the mosque to pray. Despite the danger, Roble and Keinan loved soccer. Al-Shabaab regularly swept their block. Who knew what they would do if they found boys playing the game?

Roble deflected Hooyo's warning with his infectious grin. She smiled back – she couldn't help herself – and all was well.

Amina wished that her mother loved her the way she loved Roble. She sometimes felt like there was a thick rope tensed between her and Hooyo and they were both pulling as hard as they could in opposite directions.

But she and Aabbe had always had a special relationship, similar to Fatima's warm relationship with *her* father, the prophet Mohammed. Whenever Hooyo would scold her, Aabbe would come to her rescue. Together, they shared the love of creating, which Aabbe said was close to the heart of Allah. 'Allah is the great creator,' he liked to tell Amina, 'and we are participating in his work when we make art.'

The itch crept up her fingers. She needed to get out of the house and draw on some walls. It had been several weeks since she'd finished her last work.

That was how she thought of it. *Work*. She wasn't sure if she dared to call it art. It wasn't anything like what Aabbe created. Some people, of course, would call it graffiti. But it wasn't graffiti. It wasn't random and it wasn't vandalism. It took skill and care and thought.

'Roble, will you go out and buy some vegetables so I can cook?' Hooyo asked.

'Yes, Hooyo,' Roble said. He smiled at Amina, as if to invite her along.

'Can I go, too?' Amina asked.

Hooyo and Aabbe glanced at each other. They preferred her to stay home, to leave only when she had to for school. But they were conflicted. They also wanted her to live like young women were supposed to, as they had, growing up before Somalia was plunged into perpetual war.

'Amina, it's better if you stay home,' Aabbe said.

'Where it's safe,' Hooyo added. It had been a long time since Hooyo or Ayeeyo had left the house. Ayeeyo had lived with the family all Amina's life, since Amina's grandfather had been killed when he accidentally stepped on an unexploded landmine. They hadn't even gone to mosque for several years. They had become prisoners, unwilling to leave and face the danger outside if they didn't need to.

Amina bit her lip to keep herself from protesting. She wanted to say that they weren't safe even here – wasn't the grenade that destroyed half their house proof of that? She wanted to remind them that she left the house to attend school all week long. Why was visiting the market different?

But of course she said nothing. She would save her words for the next time her schoolfriends wanted to get together.

'Let her come,' Roble said. 'Keinan will go with us and we will make sure nothing happens to her.'

Amina jumped up before her parents could say no. She grabbed a purple, floral headscarf and looked in the mirror over the front entrance. Her fingers feverish, she placed the long piece of cloth over her hair and softly folded it back, then forwards, then back again so that it looked more stylish. Keinan always looked so sharp...so cool...She tied it tightly and slipped pins on either side so that it would stay on.

Together, she and Roble stepped outside, then through the gate, stopping abruptly to let a goat walk past. It bleated weakly. A woman with a black khimar covering her head and neck nodded to greet them, then followed the goat, a long stick in her hand to keep it in line.

Amina sighed. The conflict that she always felt tugged her in different directions – the safety of home was confining, while the freedom of the streets was dangerous. She wanted both freedom and safety but she knew that was impossible.

And so she risked everything, not just to breathe the air outside of the four walls that kept her in day and night, but to use her hands to do what she knew Allah had created her to do. There was something deep inside her that needed to come out, needed to be expressed.

She had charcoal hidden in her pockets and was already thinking about how she could convince the two boys to keep watch so she could run inside one of the abandoned buildings.

Chapter 2

Amina's heart beat fast fast fast as Roble banged the tall metal gate outside Keinan's home, a few doors down the street from their own house. The two-storey house rose majestically above the wall that hedged the property and was inlaid with intricately arranged multicoloured stones. She had never been inside, although Roble went regularly to watch television, particularly if there was a soccer game on. Both boys barracked for Milan.

A woman passed by quietly, like a ghost in the long blue khimar billowing out in the wind. Street children ran past and Roble felt his pocket to make sure the money Aabbe had given him was secure.

A guard came to the gate, cracking it open to peer at them.

'We're here to see Keinan,' Roble said.

The guard nodded and disappeared behind the thick walls of Keinan's family compound. Keinan's father dealt on the black market. His family always seemed to have money.

As they stood in the street, waiting, Amina wondered if Keinan's family felt safer with a guard. She remembered visiting Aabbe's colleague, and fellow artist, Ibrahim Abdi. He also had a man guarding his front gate and electric wires strung across the top of the wall surrounding his house. Amina had felt vulnerable the entire time they were there, as though all that security made them even *more* of a target, like rats trapped in a beautiful, gilded cage. She was glad when they left. Paradoxically, she felt safer on the streets, where anything might happen.

Sometimes Amina felt homesick for a city she'd never known, a city that had died before she was even born.

Because Hooyo was a nurse and Aabbe an artist, and formerly a professor at one of Mogadishu's universities, there had been opportunities for them to leave Somalia and work elsewhere. But each time, Hooyo would say, 'If everybody who has an education or a good heart leaves, what will be left? No, this is our home and we will stay here and make our country a better place, insha'Allah, God willing.' After a few minutes, she might add, 'It is a big risk, yes, but we trust Allah will take care of us.'

Many people *had* left. People joked about how Somalis had been nomads since the beginning of time and now they were nomads in every nation of the world. 'No matter where you go, you will find Somalis there,' Aabbe liked to say.

What would Amina's life be like if her parents had made the choice to leave? Like every girl her age in Mogadishu, she had family somewhere else. Amina had many relatives in the cold parts of the world. Hooyo's youngest sister had made it to Canada and married a Somali immigrant there. Aabbe's eldest brother had fled with his wife and children to Norway. Her cousins tramped to school in the snow. *Snow!* Her uncle had said that when the wind blew, the snow looked like dirt swirling across the ground during a dust storm. But instead of the hot, stinging sand gritting across your face, snow was cold and wet and melted when it touched you.

Because they had stayed, Amina had seen just about everything – from her school's flooding after a grenade burst the water pipes to a classmate's sudden disappearance into the fiery explosion created when he stepped on a hidden landmine. Sometimes she had nightmares, but she knew better than to complain. What could Hooyo and Aabbe do about it? It was life in Mogadishu.

Still, sometimes she was jealous of her cousins' easy lives in Norway or Canada. *They* would never again face a truckload of men with guns. *They* no longer ran from danger – down alleys, through back ways, across chunks of asphalt where the street had buckled from an explosion. The sun beating down, sweat running in rivers down her arms and legs underneath her long, black dress. The worst they could complain about, living in those cold northern countries, was frostbite. Whatever *that* was.

'Roble!' Keinan banged the gate open. He bumped fists with Roble, his warm, dark eyes flashing a greeting to Amina.

She pretended to look at the street, knowing that her

13

eyes would betray her true feelings and that she probably wasn't behaving like a proper Muslim girl. But some days, she didn't worry about *being* a proper Muslim girl, as long as she *looked* proper, saying her prayers, wearing her headscarf, and reciting the Quran at dugsi, the religious classes where they memorised the holy book.

Keinan's handsome father poked his head out of the gate. He acknowledged Roble and Amina with a nod. 'Be careful out there,' he said. 'Don't wander far.' His voice was deep and gravelly. Keinan looked like his father and Amina wondered if some day he would sound like him as well.

'Yes, Aabbe,' Keinan said.

'Greet your father for me, children,' he told Roble and Amina as he closed the gate.

'Yes, adeer,' they said, addressing him with the polite term they were supposed to use when speaking to elder men.

Like always, Keinan was dressed well, in slick ironed pants and a green tunic. His clothing always showed that his father made money. Amina tried not to be jealous. Her family never had enough money. It sometimes seemed as though Aabbe would sell a painting only to turn around and use all the profit for paints for his next big project.

She had heard her father say that Abdullahi Hassan, Keinan's father, could turn a mountain of sand into a pile of gold. And it seemed he had done exactly that. He had even made a small fortune selling Aabbe's paintings. Hooyo sometimes complained that Abdullahi made more money off Aabbe's hard work than Aabbe himself – but then Aabbe would gently remind her that he was just grateful his art brought in enough money that they could survive. 'Abdullahi takes all the risk,' he'd say. 'Therefore, he should enjoy more of the profit.'

Amina walked down the street with Roble and Keinan, towards the corner where an old woman sold wilted vegetables out of a small plastic container. Roble haggled with her while Amina stared longingly across the street at a bombed-out building long since abandoned.

As they waited, Keinan whistled a tune Amina didn't recognise. She ignored him, as any good Muslim girl would. But she was *aware* of him. Her skin tingled at his closeness. She was pretty sure that feeling wasn't proper.

'I'm going to be a professional soccer player some day,' he suddenly announced.

'Yes,' Amina agreed, astonished. Keinan *was* the fastest, the sleekest, the most coordinated soccer player in the streets whenever they played.

She was always secretly eager to watch him. His skin was maariin, rich and coffee-coloured, glittering in the sun. He was thin and wiry, not muscular like Roble, but she didn't care. When he played soccer, he was *fast*. He could dart between several players, ghosting the ball right past them and kicking it through the goalposts.

Still, she was surprised that he had addressed her directly. 'Will you leave Somalia then?' Her heart skipped in beat with her hesitant words.

'Leave Somalia? Why?'

'To play soccer.'

'No. Everything I want is here.'

'But al-Shabaab has outlawed soccer.'

Keinan shook his head, scornful. He spoke loudly, as if he didn't care who might hear him. 'My father says they won't always be in power.' That was the boastful voice of privilege.

'How does your father know?' Amina's words sounded like a challenge, even though she didn't mean them that way.

'My father knows people,' Keinan said.

Amina glanced at him quickly. Of course, Keinan's father knew people. Because of his business, he knew members of the Transitional Federal Government, foreign diplomats, rich Saudis, members of the former Islamic Courts Union, leading imams, war lords. Naturally, he would know important members of al-Shabaab as well. So what did he have to fear? His powerful allies could always help him and his family. Keinan would never get into trouble for playing soccer – but Roble, the son of a political artist with no connections to powerful people, except perhaps Keinan's father, surely would. If they were ever caught.

She turned her eyes to the building opposite them, then down the streets. She could just dart across the road, draw something on one of the walls, and be back before Roble was even done bartering with the old woman.

'What are you looking at?' Keinan asked.

'That building across the street,' she said.

Without windows, the building looked like it was missing its eyes, hollow scars where the glass used to be.

Amina had seen a man with his eyes gouged out last year. Al-Shabaab soldiers had dragged the body through the streets, then cut off the man's head, dumping it outside the door to his house as a warning to the family.

'It's empty, isn't it?' Keinan asked. He looked puzzled.

Amina smiled at him. She knew she was pretty in her scarf, with her light brown eyes, dark maariin skin and white teeth. She thought it was likely that Keinan had noticed and she felt mischief stirring inside her. What if she let him in on her secret?

He smiled back at her. Something warm and intense welled up in her chest. She would show him just how talented she was. Let him see she was different from the other girls, special.

'Would you like to find out?' she dared him.

'Yes.' He seemed uncertain now, but was still willing to follow along.

When Roble had turned back towards them with a tomato and bunch of carrots in his hand, Amina ran towards the building, looking left and right to be certain nobody was watching. The boys followed, and they all darted inside the building, hiding behind one of the crumbling walls.

'We don't have time for this, Amina!' Roble said.

Roble knew all about Amina's secret art projects. He was her ally. Without him, she wouldn't be able to accomplish much since she wasn't supposed to leave the house alone.

Amina ignored Roble and started searching for the piece she had created several weeks ago. She found the mud sculpture where she'd placed it, as well as the mosaic she'd carefully arranged using broken tiles and coloured glass that she'd gathered over weeks as she went to and from school. It was a complicated design, one she'd dreamed up at night, thinking about the variety of colours and patterns she had collected – blue and green glass interspersed in a centrical pattern with black-and-white tiles scattering away from it like the rays of a sun. She wanted the broken glass to symbolise Somalian society – and for the complex pattern she had created to reveal the way that even a broken society could be put back together and made beautiful again. She had secretly borrowed Aabbe's glue to piece it together before she brought it here and left it for somebody to find.

Maybe she should take it back to Aabbe to see what he thought – she could surprise him with the work she was doing now. But she'd rather leave it here for strangers to discover – to think about, to enjoy.

She felt in her skirt for the charcoal. With a quick hand, she started sketching on the wall.

'What are you doing?' Keinan asked.

'I'm drawing a picture.'

'You're not supposed to do that! That's graffiti.'

'Try and stop her,' Roble said. He sounded both exasperated and fond – the way Hooyo sometimes expressed her frustration over Aabbe's single-minded pursuit of a painting when he was absorbed in a project.

'This building is abandoned, so nobody will care,' Amina said.

Keinan fell silent but his eyes followed Amina's hand as it whizzed up and across the wall.

She was drawing the boys playing soccer in the street. Though she had never played soccer with them, she had watched it so often from the rooftop that she felt like she was there, her feet flying, cheering as the ball went sailing through the air.

Soccer was just a game to most people but to Amina it was more than that. It was freedom. It was joy. It was the way life should be – kids playing without fear, playing despite the chaos all around them. *That* was the emotion she wanted to convey in the drawing.

'You're really good.'

She jumped when Keinan spoke, startled by the way his voice echoed loudly against the concrete walls.

Amina started to say thank you but she was cut off by Roble's sudden, flat statement. 'She's good, but she's going to get killed doing it,' he said. 'You know al-Shabaab says you're not supposed to depict the living form in art.'

'How will they ever find out about me?' Amina said.

'It's not just al-Shabaab,' Roble said. 'A lot of people say it's against Islam.'

'Not Aabbe,' Amina said.

Something crunched on the gravel just outside the room.

'What was that?' Keinan whispered.

Roble peered through the empty window. 'Al-Shabaab!' he hissed. 'Let's get out of here!'

Like cats, disturbed easily and used to leaping from

danger, Amina and Keinan sprang up and followed Roble through the abandoned building, ducking down and crawling through a window at basement level to reach the street.

Partway through the window, Amina turned her head and glimpsed a boy about Roble's age running towards her, shouting. He wore army fatigues, his face draped in a red-and-white chequered keffiyeh, the headdress revealing only his eyes. They were light brown, beautiful and earth coloured.

She scurried the rest of the way through the window and hurried after the boys as they ran through the weeds in the yard, then down a dirt alley and around the corner to Keinan's gate. He'd already reached it and the guard was opening it in response to his loud banging.

They disappeared inside and leaned against the wall, still silent, though Amina's heart was racing, faster even than when she had smiled at Keinan earlier, willing him to like her as much as she liked him.

The guard scrambled up a ladder to watch over the wall. Feet pounded against the dirt road as several men ran past.

The three teenagers peeked through the cracks in the gate. Amina relaxed only when she saw the men disappearing down the road, holding their AK-47s high.

Keinan was the first to speak, as if he were no longer afraid. 'Yeah, just try and come in here,' he yelled, though the soldiers were long gone. 'You'll see what I do if you come back here.'

'Do you have guns hidden somewhere that I haven't seen?' Roble asked. 'Or does the guard give you extra confidence?'

'Maybe.'

Amina wasn't sure if that was a twinkle in Keinan's eyes – or defiance.

Roble turned to Amina next. 'What were you *thinking*?' There was anger in his voice.

'I wanted to draw.' Amina kept her voice low, hoping he wouldn't scold her too harshly in front of Keinan. Her cheeks burned.

'You shouldn't take risks like that,' he said. 'You're putting all our lives in danger.'

'You do the same when you play soccer,' Amina shot back. 'Our lives are always in danger, but nothing will happen to us unless Allah wills it.' She had heard Ayeeyo say that and, though she wasn't certain, she tried to believe it too. 'And if that's true then what's the point in being careful? In being scared?'

'Oh, what do you know?' Roble spat on the ground.

Amina turned around, her back to the boys. She gazed at Keinan's house without seeing it. She regretted that her decision to draw on the walls of an abandoned building had led them into danger, but nobody could have predicted al-Shabaab soldiers would show up exactly when they had.

'Have you looked at her drawings, Roble?' Keinan asked. 'She's really good.' He pumped his fists in the air. 'Almost as good as I am at playing soccer.'

Amina found herself smiling at him with abandon.

Nobody could resist Keinan, not even Hooyo – even when he was being cheeky.

Still, she'd never smile at him like that if her parents or Ayeeyo were around.

'You're such a liar, man,' Roble said, laughing. 'And you know I'm better than you any day.'

The two jostled each other.

'Anyway, so what if she's good?' Roble asked, suddenly sober. 'Is it worth our lives? Do you want to *die*, just because Amina likes to draw?'

'You don't keep a gift like that to yourself,' Keinan argued. 'It would be a crime, just like it's a crime not to admit *I'm* the best soccer player.' He grinned again, and added, 'Amina, I hope you keep drawing.'

'Thanks.' Amina whispered, afraid she might start crying if she spoke in her regular voice.

'Come on, Amina. Let's go home,' Roble said. He looked disappointed. Was it because Keinan had encouraged her to keep drawing? Or was it because Amina liked to break the rules?

As she followed him out of Keinan's yard and into the dusty street, she resolved to be better in the future. She could be more careful. And she could make smaller pieces in her own yard, then leave them where somebody might find them. She used to think she created street art because that was the only avenue open to her. Now she knew she craved that public expression, the possibility that when people saw her work, it might change how they thought about the world.

Roble and Amina looked left and right at the now

empty street and hurried to their own gate, just a few doors away.

Roble closed the gate behind them and secured it with the heavy metal lock Aabbe had added for more security. It clanked into place.

Locked in. She was safe and secure. Nobody could get in but neither could Amina leave, unless somebody – usually Roble or Aabbe – accompanied her.

Her shoulders sagged.

Chapter 3

Like always, Roble was waiting for Amina outside school beside a squat mango tree bursting with oval fruit still waiting to ripen.

Hooyo and Aabbe insisted that they go to school unless a battle was raging. Then nobody went anywhere and they'd crouch on the floor as bullets whizzed overhead. On normal days, school started early in the morning and ended at noon. Afterwards, they went to dugsi, to memorise the Quran and learn what they needed to know to be a good Muslim.

'Will we see you later?' Filad called after Amina as she started to run to join Roble and Keinan. 'After dugsi we'll get together with all the girls and have a showdown.'

Sometimes at school the girls ignored her, but they were always nice to her when they wanted her to come to a competition. She was a good poet. Her team always won.

'If Ayeeyo lets me, I'll come,' Amina said.

'We'll fetch you,' Basra said. 'Then she won't say no.'

'After dugsi, then,' Amina said.

'What took you so long?' Roble grumbled. 'We can't be late or the teacher will beat us.'

She ignored him and greeted them the proper way. 'Asalaam alaykum, peace be upon you,' she said, glancing at Keinan from beneath her eyelashes, pulse racing when she saw how he stared at her.

'Wa 'alaykum asalaam, and peace be upon you as well,' Keinan said.

'The teacher will probably beat you anyway,' Amina told Roble. 'Have you memorised the Quran yet?'

'*I* have it memorised,' Keinan interrupted.

'All right, hotshot, then why do you still go to dugsi?' Roble asked.

Keinan shrugged. 'For fun.'

Roble hooted. Nobody went to dugsi for fun. It was just what you had to do – that was all.

Amina dropped her eyes to the dirt. Keinan was still staring at her. She was glad he went to the same dugsi, even though they sat on opposite sides of the classroom – Amina with the girls, Keinan with the boys, all of them sitting uncomfortably on the floor. Amina's back always ached after dugsi.

She walked alongside them quietly as Roble opened his book and started quizzing Keinan on different suras, chapters in the Quran. Keinan was smooth, the holy words rolling off his tongue. No matter what verse Roble asked him to recite, he knew it by heart.

'Have you really already memorised the entire Quran?' Roble asked.

Keinan grinned. 'Yes!'

'How did you do it?'

'I'm just *that* good,' Keinan said.

'No, really, I want to know how you did it,' Roble said.

'When I was younger, my teacher tied me to the chair and wouldn't let me leave until I could recite the portion he wanted me to learn that day,' Keinan explained. 'And that is how I memorised it.'

Amina was quietly horrified. She and Roble exchanged glances.

'What?' Keinan said. He looked from Amina to Roble. 'At least I learned it.'

'Aabbe doesn't think our teachers should beat us,' Amina said. 'Not at school, not at dugsi.'

'What's he going to do about it?' Keinan asked. 'All the teachers do it.'

He was right. And even though Aabbe was opposed to corporal punishment, they knew they would never receive sympathy at home. Hooyo said the teacher wouldn't beat them if they did what they were supposed to do. 'You won't be afraid if you've learned your verses,' she liked to say. But Hooyo wasn't there. She didn't know that some teachers had favourites, and they might pick on you no matter how hard you tried. At their dugsi, the teacher would sometimes blindfold students who hadn't learned their lessons and allow the other children to pinch them. They hadn't told Hooyo that.

The boys started talking about Somaliland, the area to the north that had declared independence from Somalia back in 1991, when the country first fell into civil war. Somalia refused to recognise its sovereignty. It was often a more peaceful region than other parts of the country.

'Some people say Somaliland has the happiest people in the world,' Roble said.

'Yeah, because the men chew khat all day long,' Keinan joked. Khat was a herbal drug that some men chewed because it gave them brief bursts of euphoria. It stained their teeth green and sometimes made their eyes red. 'If we did that all day, every day, in Mogadishu, we'd be happy too.'

The streets rang with their boisterous laughter. They had reached dugsi in a good mood but quieted down quickly and went inside silently, as they were supposed to do. As Amina turned to sit with the girls, she caught Keinan's eye.

She sat down, her brain hazy with a happy glow, determined that even the teacher's bad mood wouldn't rob her of this.

◆━━◆

Amina's schoolfriends showed up at her house after dugsi, just as they'd promised. They knocked on the gate and Amina told them to wait while she asked Hooyo if she could join them.

'We won't wait long!' Filad warned.

'Oh, don't say that,' Basra said. Amina had always liked her even though they'd never become close. Basra was already so busy with other friends. 'You know Amina's the best poetry writer. We'll wait as long as we need to. I want her on my team!' She smiled at Amina and Amina hurried inside, happy that one of the girls really wanted her to come along.

Usually, Hooyo was a busy mother, cooking, cleaning, organising Aabbe's studio as much as he would allow. She rarely stopped. She liked to keep active, now that she wasn't working – a decision she had made because it was too dangerous to go back and forth to the hospital every day. But now, like most days, Amina found her sitting by the window, reading a book. The baby growing in her belly had made her tired and moody.

Amina sat beside her, hoping she was happy right now. 'Hooyo, some of my classmates are outside wanting to know if I can go to Filad's house for a while.'

Hooyo put her book down. She looked at Amina, slightly exasperated. 'You should stay home, here, like a good girl,' she said.

Amina waited to see how this would play out.

'Always running around, playing with your friends.' Hooyo clucked her tongue. 'You are old enough to be married. Men don't want a wild woman, always going here, always going there, never staying home.'

Amina silently appealed to her grandmother.

'Khadija, you know Amina is a good girl,' Ayeeyo said. 'She's not wild, she's just spending time with other girls. You had more freedom when you were a girl than she does now.'

'I had more freedom, yes,' Hooyo said. 'But Mogadishu was safe then.'

'What was it like?' Amina asked.

'Oh! It was so serene and beautiful, before the war,' Hooyo said, her voice wistful. 'You have no idea what it looked like before so many buildings were bombed and started falling apart. We had the best architecture in the world – inspired by Islam and styles like you find in Iraq, Turkey and Italy.'

'I wish I could have seen it,' Amina said. She sometimes caught glimpses of the architectural beauty of pre-war Mogadishu, but it was rare.

'I wish that as well,' Hooyo said. 'It was safe to walk the streets then. Some women were quite daring in the way they dressed.'

'Did they wear headscarfs?' Amina asked. She had heard from her cousins that some Muslim women in other parts of the world didn't have to cover their hair when they left the house.

'Some women did not,' Hooyo said. 'Some women even wore trousers – like men!'

Amina couldn't imagine that.

'Oh, tell her the truth, Khadija,' Ayeeyo said. '*You* were one of those daring women.'

Hooyo sighed. 'Yes. I loved this city when I was young. There were movie theatres and restaurants and it was safe to go sailing in the ocean.'

Amina tried to imagine her mother, young and glamourous, going sailing on a sunny spring day.

Mogadishu was nothing like that now, of course. Women didn't have so much freedom.

'You should let her go, Khadija,' Ayeeyo said. 'Her fate is already written by Allah. If she stays here just to be safe, she may meet danger right here in her own house.'

'Besides,' Amina said, 'I don't want to get married yet so who cares if men think I'm a little wild? I want to finish school and go to college, like you.'

Hooyo gazed at her daughter. In a rare gesture of fondness, she reached out and smoothed Amina's headscarf. 'I suppose you're right,' she said. 'Amina, you may go, but be careful.'

'Thank you, Hooyo!' Amina was already running towards the front door.

'And don't go *near* a boy,' Hooyo called after her. 'Remember, if you touch a boy, you'll have a seizure and die.'

'Very funny, Hooyo!' Amina laughed.

'Why are you laughing? I'm serious. That's exactly what will happen.' But Hooyo was smiling. It was a joke, yet she meant it all the same.

The girls walked in a small group, seven altogether, to Filad's house. Amina's parents allowed her to go with the girls as long as they stayed in a group. There was safety in numbers, Aabbe had told Amina, though even a group wasn't entirely safe either. They looked like a rainbow walking down the street, each girl wearing a different colour headscarf. Amina was relieved when Basra fell into place beside her. Since the other girls were all good friends at school, she would normally have been the odd one out.

Filad and Basra couldn't have been more different,

even though they were the natural leaders of the group. Filad was short and curvy, a few curly tendrils poking out of her purple headscarf, with a plain face and a bossy manner. Basra was tall and slender and very pretty, funny and loud, although she sometimes looked a little sad. The two girls had been friends for a long time and Amina was a little jealous of the easy way they related to each other. She wished she had a good friend like that.

Filad's loud voice rang out over the girls' chatter. 'Did you guys hear the news?'

'No. What?' Dhuuxo asked.

Basra chimed in, 'Do you mean the news about Hodan getting married?'

Amina felt sick. Hodan was only fifteen. Though she herself liked Keinan, she wasn't ready to get married.

Other girls liked growing up. It was just one more thing that made Amina feel different. A year ago, when the girls were thirteen, one of Amina's classmates had to leave school and get married. Amina remembered going to the mosque for the ceremony and doing the traditional buraanbur with the other women at the wedding – stamping her feet, clapping, singing, trilling. She had eaten an entire plate of halwa, the candied jelly slipping spoonful by delicious spoonful from her tongue down into her belly. Then she'd suffered half the night with cramps because Hooyo and Ayeeyo didn't normally let her indulge in such rich food.

'Hodan! Getting married!' the other girls exclaimed. 'When?'

Filad looked disappointed that Basra had stolen her news but she recovered quickly. 'She's getting married next week and her husband is taking her to Kenya.'

'So she's leaving the country?' Dhuuxo asked. 'Lucky her!'

'Does she already have family in Kenya?' Saafi asked.

'Her husband's parents and sister are already in Nairobi,' Basra explained.

'Wow, she's really starting a new life,' Saafi said. 'I wouldn't want to leave my mother. I need her.'

'Yeah, you need her,' teased Basra. 'You need her because you don't know how to cook and no Somali man wants a wife who can't cook.'

Saafi joined in the laughter at her expense. 'Yes,' she admitted. 'I would always be running home to ask Hooyo how to make dinner.'

The girls kept chattering about the news and Amina let the words float above her head, just out of reach of her ears. She ran her hand along the cement walls as they passed. Concrete was such a strong material, yet still so vulnerable to bombs and guns.

'Have you ever been to Filad's house?' Basra asked.

'No,' Amina said.

'Don't tell Filad, but when I was a little girl, I was scared of her mother.' She kept her voice low but a grin on her face suggested that she wasn't really sharing a secret.

'Why?' Amina's restless eyes scanned the row of houses as they passed. This was a neighbourhood she had never marked with her work. She saw several buildings that looked abandoned and presented luring possibilities. She noted the blue tiles lacing the walls of one house with a flat roof. Maybe she could borrow just a tiny bit of blue paint and Aabbe wouldn't notice.

'You'll see. She has really long ears and I thought she was the dhaagdheer.' Basra erupted with laughter and Amina joined in. The dhaagdheer was a woman with excessively long ears who took children at night and ate them. As long as you were home before dark, you would be safe.

'I used to run away whenever I saw people with long ears,' Amina admitted, 'even after Hooyo told me the dhaagdheer wasn't real.'

'Oh, not my hooyo,' Basra said. 'My hooyo used to scare me with lots of stories. But then, when my sister died, I realised there were scarier things in the streets of Mogadishu than anything Hooyo ever mentioned.'

'Your sister died?' Amina asked. 'I'm so sorry to hear that! What happened?'

Basra paused for a second, then said, 'She was murdered.'

Amina stumbled, reaching for a tall palm tree to steady herself. She looked at her classmate out of the corners of her eyes. How terrible! Why did Basra seem so calm?

'So now I don't see the point of being scared of the dhaagdheer.'

'Are you scared of *any*thing?'

Basra considered this. 'Not really, no.'

'You're really brave. If my sister had been murdered…'

'It was a long time ago,' Basra said matter-of-factly.

'You can't stop bad things from happening. You just have to keep on living.'

Amina was amazed. She thought about all the things that frightened her: being killed, being kidnapped by al-Shabaab and forced to become the wife of a soldier, losing her family. She didn't think she could be as calm as Basra.

'But, after it happened, I cried for months,' Basra admitted. 'A river of tears! Sometimes I still cry. You never stop missing someone you love.'

◆➤■◆

At Filad's house, the girls gathered in the living room. Filad's mother served sweet cinnamon tea in pretty white cups, blue flowers etched along the edges. Amina sank her feet into the thick Persian rugs covering the floor, relishing the softness between her toes.

Quickly, they broke up into teams. Sometimes, they pitted one neighbourhood against another. One group would compose a poem and recite it – something lightly teasing and derogatory about the other neighbourhood or extolling their own neighbourhood's virtues, or talking about what it meant to be Somali. Then the other group would counter it with their own poem. Today, Filad said two team leaders would choose the girls on their team.

'I'll be one team leader and Basra will be the other team leader,' Filad said.

Nobody argued with her. They always did what Filad said.

Amina was Basra's first choice. She joined Basra, flushed with pleasure to be selected so early.

When all the girls had been selected for one team or another, they settled back onto opposite sides of the living room. All the girls had been competing like this, writing and reciting poetry most of their lives. It was second nature to Amina and she loved it.

It was the other group's turn first. Filad stepped up and began reciting a poem with a strong, rhythmic beat.

Girls of Mogadishu
We have grit, we have courage
Let's fight it out

Amina listened to Filad chant and looked at all the girls gathered together in the room. They were so pretty. She had never heard Basra's story before but she knew Filad had also lost a brother and cousins. What sadness did the other girls hide behind their smiles?

Filad finished and sat down, crowing loudly. 'Now, let's see what you girls can do,' she told Basra's group.

Amina jumped to her feet to go first. Lines of poetry were already forming in her head because of Basra's story about her sister.

She began to chant the poem she had just created.

When the sun falls from the sky
And lies broken on the city street
What is left to fear?
We've lost much but we've survived
We are true Somalis.

The girls listened, nodding their heads and smiling. Amina could see their respect for her skill, even from the girls on Filad's team. But she could also see the way they responded to the words. One girl nodded her head when Amina repeated the line, 'What is left to fear?' That girl had a story to tell. Everybody in the room had a story to tell.

Everyone but Amina.

As she stood there reciting, she realised she had been lucky all of her life. She had relatives living in all corners of the world, but except for her grandfather, Awoowe, who had died before she was even born, she had never lost a single family member to the war.

◆▬◆

Roble came to fetch Amina early in the evening. They walked home together in the cool evening, a refreshing breeze blowing salt air from the ocean. Before going inside, Amina stopped by Aabbe's studio, knocking gently on the door. His eyes were bright and alert when he opened it so she knew it was a good time to interrupt. 'Come in,' he invited.

She sat on the high stool he used when painting and twirled around on it, as though she were a little girl, telling him about her afternoon. She revelled in the details of the poetry competition, how she had beaten every girl in the room with the power of her words.

'Ah-ha, you are a true Somali girl.' Aabbe laughed, his deep, hearty laugh, the one she loved. 'We Somalis, we are nothing but poetry and camels, camels and poetry.'

She joined in, partly because of the joke and partly because it was impossible not to laugh when Aabbe did.

Amina sometimes wondered whether she would be jealous if Hooyo's baby was another little girl. What if Aabbe loved the baby more than he loved her?

'We used to court girls with poetry,' Aabbe told her. 'We boys would make arrangements to meet after all the parents had gone to bed. Then we would go somewhere and make a big bonfire. If a girl looked outside and saw the bonfire, she knew she was being called to join us. And so the girls would come and we would meet them at the fire – the boys on one side and the girls on the other. And we would sing a song or recite poetry, and the girls would sing a song or recite poetry, and we would go back and forth like that. That was how we wooed. A boy had to convince a girl he could write poetry if he was going to win her heart.'

'And your parents didn't know you were sneaking out to meet girls?'

'Of course they knew,' Aabbe said. 'We boys did it because our fathers told us that was what they did. They knew what we were doing in general, but never the specific night.'

'So were you good at writing poetry?'

'Sadly, no. But if the poetry didn't work, we boys would wrestle each other. And I was very good at wrestling.'

Amina couldn't help giggling at the picture of her father reciting bad poetry in front of a bonfire and then wrestling a boy, all to win the heart of a girl. 'You were real country boys,' Amina said. 'The boys in Mogadishu would never do something like that.'

'Yes, Roble and Keinan would probably sneer at how innocent we were.' Aabbe sighed.

'So, did you win Hooyo because you wrestled another boy for her?' Amina teased.

'I knocked another boy out with one pop to the face,' Aabbe joked, mimicking the pop with his fist. Then he said, more seriously, 'We met our first year in college. She was so beautiful and capable and smart. I knew she could do anything she wanted to if she just set her mind to it. Like you, Amina. You have that same crazy determination.'

'Why is it crazy? Is that a bad thing?'

'It's wonderful,' Aabbe said. 'It's only crazy because you're a girl, growing up in Somalia. In most parts of the world, you would be rewarded for it. Here? Here, you know yourself it's a liability.'

Everybody knew that al-Shabaab was opposed to women's education. Even though lots of Somalis secretly disagreed with al-Shabaab, people were too afraid to do anything about it. Lots of girls had dropped out of school and Amina had learned to keep her mouth shut so she wouldn't get in trouble. But underneath her quietness lay a seething mass of ideas she was just waiting to express.

'I wish Somalia could go back to the way it was before the war,' she said. 'It seemed … simpler. Nicer.'

'Don't look back, Amina,' Aabbe said. 'And don't get stuck in the here and now. Just keep looking ahead, no matter what.'

Chapter 4

Amina sat beside Ayeeyo on the joodari they slept on together and gently played with her curly, silvery-grey hair. The bedroom was small but at least she didn't have to sleep in the front room like Roble.

Amina's stomach growled. It was the first day of Ramadan so she hadn't had anything to eat or drink since dawn. She wouldn't be able to eat or drink anything again until the sun set. But as hard as the month would be, the sacrifice helped her remember what she was doing and why, and made her long to be pure and right with Allah.

She wondered if she should feel bad about talking to Keinan. But she didn't.

'Ayeeyo,' she said now that they were alone. 'Why are Aabbe and Hooyo so afraid? They keep talking, all day and all night long.'

Ayeeyo didn't respond.

For the past two days, when they weren't working or praying, Hooyo and Aabbe had spent their time talking urgently in deep whispers. They fell silent whenever Amina came close.

Amina thought perhaps Ayeeyo might tell her what was going on because she, too, seemed worried. She watched Hooyo and Aabbe's conversations like a scared chicken, about to start running to avoid the chopping block.

'Is something wrong with the baby?' Amina tried again.

Ayeeyo pressed her lips together and shook her head.

'Then what's wrong?'

'It's nothing, my butterfly. Don't worry your little heart.'

But Amina could see the fear in her eyes.

She left the bedroom, crossed the front room and opened the door, looking for Roble. A blast of humid air greeted her, sucking away her breath.

Roble stood inside the gate talking to Keinan. Amina grabbed her headscarf and quickly covered her hair, winding it around and tucking the ends in so it was secure.

Keinan glanced up and their eyes met. She launched herself down the stone steps and hurried across the yard.

'What are you doing?' she asked Roble.

He hooted at her. 'What does it look like? Talking to my friend.'

'Have you had any adventures lately?' Keinan greeted her. 'Have you created anything for the world to marvel at?'

Amina glanced back at the house, wondering if Hooyo or Ayeeyo were watching. 'No,' she answered. 'We have come and gone from school without stopping. Roble said I must give up my street art.'

She spoke lightly so she wouldn't betray the heaviness she felt over Roble's decision. Her intentions had been good, she knew, and Allah honoured intentions, not the outcome of your actions, which you could never predict. But for Roble, the difference didn't matter. Her actions had put them in danger.

'That's too bad,' Keinan said. 'We will be your lookout, if Roble changes his mind.'

Amina looked at Roble. She knew there was pleading in her eyes and it made her feel weak. She hated being dependent on another person. She lowered her eyes.

'Maybe next week, Amina,' Roble said.

'Thank you,' she said, and even though she wanted to hide it, she couldn't keep the note of joy out of her voice. 'What about you, Keinan? Has the best soccer player done anything marvellous lately?' she asked.

'Unlike you, I don't need to create marvels,' Keinan joked. '*I'm* the work of art!'

She joined the boys in their rowdy laughter, and, for a moment, Amina felt her parents' worry draining out of her. It made her brave enough to broach the subject, even though Keinan was there. 'Roble, what's wrong? Why are Hooyo and Aabbe so worried all the time?'

Roble glanced at Keinan.

'You can tell me,' Amina said, wondering why Roble seemed so uneasy. 'Is it the baby?'

'I don't know how much I should say.' Roble spoke in a low voice, even though they were inside the gate, behind the thick walls that protected the family from soldiers of all kinds.

'I can keep a secret,' Amina said.

'Me too,' Keinan said.

Roble hesitated. 'We aren't sure exactly,' he said, finally, 'but there are rumours that somebody in al-Shabaab has offered a reward for anyone who brings Aabbe to them. He's already received several death threats in the last few days.'

It felt as though a sharp stick had punctured Amina's lungs. It was suddenly hard to breathe.

Keinan asked the question she couldn't voice. 'But why would al-Shabaab want to kill your father?'

'Because of his paintings,' Roble whispered. 'They say his paintings are un-Islamic because they depict the living form. They say that his paintings inspire Somalis to rebel against the true teachings of Allah, especially Somalis in the diaspora, because they are already surrounded by infidels.'

'They think *all* art is haram,' Keinan said. 'It's not just your father's paintings that are forbidden.'

Amina whispered, too, as though even the walls might harbour an enemy. 'But everybody knows where to find him,' she said. 'They could raid the neighbourhood. Al-Shabaab has soldiers. If they want to kill him, why don't they just come here to fetch him?' As soon as she said it, she wanted to snatch the words back. It *was* too easy. What if they figured that out?

'I don't know.' Roble's eyes flitted to Keinan again and again, and Amina found herself wondering why. Since Keinan's father knew everybody, including al-Shabaab, was he protecting her father? Or did that connection put Aabbe in even greater danger? She wished that thought hadn't occurred to her.

'Aabbe should leave,' she said.

'Where would he go?' Roble asked.

The answer was obvious. 'Somewhere safe,' she said.

Roble whooped. 'And where is that?'

Amina had to admit that she couldn't think of a safe place in the whole city. The Transitional Federal Government was so weak it offered no protection. It seemed like al-Shabaab was everywhere and that meant that everywhere was dangerous. That's why Hooyo and Ayeeyo refused to leave the house.

Of course, al-Shabaab wasn't really everywhere. Not anymore. Earlier that summer, African Union soldiers had successfully taken back some of the territory al-Shabaab held, including Bakaara Market. That meant there were places that might be safe for the time being – but it was impossible to predict whether they would remain safe, since al-Shabaab would eventually try to gain back that territory for itself.

'Maybe the airport is safe,' Amina said. After all, the airport was patrolled by a heavily armed securities company, hired by the Transitional Federal Government, not al-Shabaab. And if Aabbe was at the airport, he might have a chance to actually leave. Go to Kenya first, then seek asylum in Australia or America. Surely Aabbe would get asylum. But if he left, she would want to go with him. She wouldn't want to be left behind.

'He could come stay with us,' Keinan said. 'My house is safe.'

'What, because of all those secret guns you have stashed away?' Roble scoffed.

'What guns?' Amina asked.

Keinan looked uncomfortable. 'He's just talking. My house is safe because we have a guard, not guns.'

'The guard has a gun,' Amina said.

'On the streets, you know, they say your family has a secret connection to al-Shabaab.' Roble's voice shook. 'If we send Aabbe to your house, are we sending him to the lions?'

'What do you mean?' Keinan said, as though Roble's words had wounded him.

The neighbourhood muezzin's voice rose in a long, high wail to call the faithful for prayer.

'We have to go,' Roble muttered.

Keinan slipped out of the gate, a hurt look on his face, while Amina and Roble hurried inside to join their own family.

◆━■━◆

'It sounded like you were accusing Keinan of something,' Amina said. 'Are you angry with him?'

Roble was performing his ablutions, washing his face, hands and feet with a basin of water in the kitchen. 'I don't know.'

'You must know,' Amina persisted.

'Forget it,' he said. 'It's not important.'

'How can you say that?' Amina said. 'We were talking about people who want to kill Aabbe.' She didn't want to believe that their neighbours would

44

betray them. But these days, you could trust no-one.

Roble sighed. 'I'm not angry at Keinan. He's my friend. But I don't trust his father.'

Amina took the basin and threw the dirty water out the back door as Roble hurried to join Aabbe. They would go pray at the mosque with the other men while Amina would stay at home and pray with Hooyo and Ayeeyo.

She filled the basin with water while she thought. Then she, too, washed her face, hands and feet, and went to the little alcove off the front room, where Hooyo and Ayeeyo were already facing Mecca, their heads covered with long white cloths. Ayeeyo sat on a chair, unable to kneel completely because of the arthritis in her knees. The sun shone through the paned window and flooded Ayeeyo's face in blue light.

Amina unfurled her sijaayad, following Hooyo's smooth motions as she raised her hands in supplication, bending down to the knees, rising again, then kneeling prone and stretching her arms out towards the wall. Amina remembered how when she was younger Aabbe would sometimes stay home to pray. He would hold her next to him on his sijaayad. She missed that.

Amina noticed a special urgency in Hooyo's voice as she prayed and she thought back to what Roble had told her. How could anybody think her father's work was un-Islamic? *If they only knew him*, she thought, *then they would know that he's fully submissive to the will of Allah.*

It was Allah's work he was doing, he always said. It was important to remind the people of Somalia that the path of peace was a righteous one. His message was folded into the layers of oil that he used to paint the picture of ocean waves. How could anybody be opposed to his desire for the people of the country to lay down the sword so that they could be at peace? Who wanted the endless bloodshed? Who wanted to kill her father? Maybe a lot of people in Somalia didn't want to hear his message.

She tried to focus her mind on prayer but her throat ached. Tears welled up in her eyes but she willed them not to spill over. She had to be strong. She couldn't show Hooyo that she knew something was wrong. She bent low at the waist, kept her eyes on the ground and prayed that she could be strong and pretend that she knew nothing.

◆❯❰◆

After prayers, Hooyo sent Amina to the kitchen to help Ayeeyo prepare food for the evening's feast.

Cooking during Ramadan was a special trial, especially at the beginning of the month, like today, when she still had to get used to going all day without food or drink. Amina chopped onions and tomatoes methodically, her mouth watering. She swished spit around in her mouth, *patah patah patah*, trying to ignore the hunger pains.

Ayeeyo heated oil inside a clay pot perched precariously on a bed of live coals. She dropped the onions in and they sizzled, the oil popping up in tiny hot spurts. Amina smiled at Ayeeyo. This was what she liked best about her grandmother. The two of them could be perfectly silent together but Amina never felt alone.

A sudden, loud rapping at the front door startled Ayeeyo so badly she jerked, knocking the pot which teetered off the coals. Amina hurried to pick up the onions off the floor, the hot oil scalding her hands.

'How did somebody get inside the gate?' Hooyo asked, appearing in the kitchen doorway. 'Did you leave it unlocked, Amina?' Hooyo didn't wait for an answer. She draped a khimar around her head as she hurried to the front door.

Anger pinched Amina's chest. Why did Hooyo always blame her? She wasn't the one who had just left to go pray at the mosque, but Hooyo would never blame her precious Roble or Aabbe.

Amina followed Hooyo closely. Ayeeyo stayed behind in the kitchen doorway, holding a dishcloth as though it were a weapon.

'Who is here?' Hooyo called through the door.

The man had a harsh and authoritative voice. 'We are here for Samatar Omar Khalid.'

'Who are you?' Hooyo asked.

'We are here for Samatar Omar Khalid,' the man repeated.

'He isn't here,' Hooyo said. She stood with her ear to the door, as though she could hear what they were thinking if she pressed against it hard enough.

'Where is he?'

'He isn't here,' Hooyo repeated, her voice shaking as though it were cold. 'He went to mosque for prayers.'

She had wound the edge of her scarf around her hand and was biting the cloth between her teeth. Saliva soaked through the folds.

It was only then that Amina realised just how afraid Hooyo was. She tiptoed forward and crouched beside her mother, putting her hand on Hooyo's arm. It trembled beneath her touch.

'We must check the house,' the man said. 'We will not go away until you let us in.'

Hooyo stayed perfectly still and silent, leaning with her ear against the door. Amina wondered what she was thinking.

'Let them search the house, Hooyo,' she whispered finally. 'Aabbe isn't here.'

So Hooyo unlocked the door. Several men with long beards and chequered keffiyehs shouldered their way through. Amina recognised the uniform – al-Shabaab soldiers.

The soldiers quickly swept the house, checking every room and every closet. The commander, the man who was clearly in charge, stayed near Hooyo and Amina at the front door, waiting, his finger on the trigger of the AK-47 he carried.

Amina leaned against Hooyo, hoping he wouldn't notice her.

The ceiling echoed with the sounds of the soldiers shuffling around on the second floor. A few seconds later, they returned, coming down the stairs.

'He isn't here,' one of them announced.

The commander scrutinised Hooyo as he bent his

head towards one of the soldiers. They conferred in low voices. 'Tell your husband we'll return,' he said. 'We have a few things to discuss.'

'Yes, of course,' Hooyo said.

Amina was amazed. How could Hooyo sound so cheerful, so unworried? Yet one look at her eyes and Amina could see it was all a lie.

The men murmured for a few more seconds, then marched out of the house and towards the gate.

'Please, Amina, look out the window to see if they're gone,' Hooyo whispered.

It wasn't until Amina confirmed that the men were gone that Hooyo moved. And when she moved, she was fast, like an ocean wave with a strong undertow pulling Amina out into dangerous waters. 'Hurry, hurry,' she hissed. 'Go to the mosque. Get your father. Tell him to come. He must leave here, he must. I am packing his things already.'

'Where will he go?' Amina asked. But Hooyo was already running to their bedroom, her bare feet pitter-pattering against the tiles. She turned once to look at Amina, frozen by the window.

'Go!' she screamed. 'Go!'

Amina jumped up and unlocked the door. She hurtled across the yard, scuttling through the rubble, stopping short when she noticed the door to Aabbe's studio flung wide open.

The men had clearly visited the studio first. They had scattered art supplies here and there. One of Aabbe's paintings lay face down in the centre of the room, ripped through the middle. Amina stared at it for a minute, wild thoughts flashing through her mind.

Another painting, one Aabbe had clearly been working on that very day, depicted Bakaara Market, alive with people haggling over prices. A little girl sat in the corner playing with stones while her mother sold cloth. A street child hid behind a bright red cloth, sneaking a hand into the pocket of a man making a purchase. Pigeons hopped around on one foot near the food sellers. A mosque towered over the market in the distant background, almost comically large in comparison to the rest of the scene. In the foreground, three or four men exchanged parcels secretly, even as guns spilled out of them. The guns were also absurdly large, as big as the mosque itself.

It was paintings like this that had got him into trouble. They were the reason for the death threats. Not just because he depicted the living form – but because his art revealed the men who made war and sold guns as hypocrites, trading their weapons of death in the shadow of the mosque. 'It isn't Allah's will that we Muslims should kill each other,' Aabbe liked to say.

Amina rushed from the studio and ran out of the gate. She looked up and down the street to see if the men were nearby but they had already gone. She ran towards the nearby mosque, where she knew Aabbe and Roble liked to pray.

She saw them coming from a long way away, walking silently together, and she suddenly realised Roble looked like a man beside Aabbe. She stopped for a minute, taking a snapshot of the scene in her head.

She would paint this scene some day, her father and her brother walking home from the nearby mosque through Mogadishu's rubble, a large bird circling overhead, the brilliant blue sky.

They saw her then and sprinted towards her. She plunged towards them until they met in the middle.

'Is something wrong with Hooyo?' Aabbe demanded as soon as he reached her.

'She's fine,' Amina gasped. 'But you need to come home now. Quick!'

They ran together, clanging the gate and whirling up the steps to the front door, inside, and across the front room. They stood at the door of Hooyo and Aabbe's bedroom.

Hooyo and Ayeeyo were running around the bedroom with a half-packed bag of clothes and food.

'Samatar,' Hooyo said. She flew across the bedroom, wretched in her fear. 'They have come for you. You must go.'

'Where will he go?' Amina asked.

Her words fell into the thick silence and nobody answered.

Aabbe took Hooyo's hands in his and raised them to his lips. He kissed them and placed one on each cheek, his hands covering hers. He repeated Amina's words. 'My heart, where will I go?'

Tears streamed down Hooyo's cheeks. 'To your brother's,' she said.

'I am sure they have already been there,' Aabbe said, 'and they will return.'

'Go to Ibrahim's house,' Roble said. 'He's your friend. He'll help you.'

Amina watched her father carefully as he considered Roble's suggestion then rejected it.

'They will go there also,' he said.

'You know what will happen when they come back,' Hooyo said. Her shoulders were already sinking in regret and frustration.

'I don't know what will happen,' Aabbe said. 'Insha'Allah, God willing, perhaps they will forget all about me.'

'Are you talking about al-Shabaab, Aabbe?' Amina asked, though she already knew what his answer would be. 'Are they looking for you because of your paintings?'

Aabbe placed a hand tenderly on her arm. 'Yes, Amina. They have decided I am a threat to their version of Islam.'

Ayeeyo came forward now. 'Son,' she said. 'Son, you should listen to your wife. If you go, there is a chance you will escape.'

'A chance, Hooyo,' Aabbe said to his mother, 'but also the chance that I will fall into even worse hands.'

'Worse than al-Shabaab?' Roble asked.

'You know what it's like out there,' Aabbe said. 'There is nowhere safe, not unless Allah wills it. No, let's pray and hope for the best.'

He turned as if to go to the small alcove where the family liked to pray. But his motion was interrupted when the front door banged open. The soldiers who had come earlier looking for Aabbe had returned.

Amina shrank back against the wall.

Roble stood in their path, as though to protect Aabbe, but one of the soldiers took the butt of his AK-47 and slammed it into his face. Roble's entire body smacked against the wall. He slumped to the floor, unconscious.

All three men crossed the room. One held a machine gun to Ayeeyo's head and another to Hooyo's chest. The third seized Aabbe. They were shouting, all at once, and it was impossible to understand what they were saying.

Ayeeyo cried out, 'Don't hurt an old woman, I beg you.' She bent over, crying, hiding her face. The man jerked her by the arm and thrust her into the kitchen. He joined the man holding on to Aabbe and pointed his gun at Aabbe's forehead.

Hooyo was openly sobbing. The man grabbed her arm roughly. 'Please,' she cried. 'Leave him. Can't you see he's needed? What will we do if you take him?'

'Shut up!' The man holding her swung his gun around the room, finally pointing it at Amina. 'Infidels have no rights.'

'No!' Aabbe said. 'Leave my daughter alone! I'm the person you want.'

Silent and swift, the two men holding Aabbe dragged him across the tiles and outside the house. The remaining man continued to point the gun at Amina as he released Hooyo and backed up, following them.

The door slammed shut behind them. The sound reverberated and echoed through the house, suddenly cavernous and empty.

Amina's legs felt wobbly and she stared at the door

from where Aabbe had disappeared. She could only watch as Ayeeyo ran to Roble's side, bending over and putting a hand over his mouth.

'Thank Allah, he's breathing,' Ayeeyo said.

Hooyo began to wail.

But Amina's eyes were dry. She couldn't believe it. Aabbe's disappearance was so sudden, it seemed impossible that it had even happened.

Chapter 5

Hooyo and Ayeeyo argued after the men left, the house tense with the sound of their bickering.

Hooyo was convinced they should stay put until they could find out what had happened to Aabbe, while Ayeeyo said, 'No, Khadija, we must leave Somalia and go somewhere safe. We have lost enough by staying here.'

'I may be Somali, but I'm not a nomad,' Hooyo said.

Amina listened to them argue. They repeated the same ideas over and over, neither one changing their mind, neither one listening to the other.

They were sitting in the front room. The sun had set but nobody had eaten. Dinner had long since burned and then cooled. Amina's stomach rumbled but she didn't dare mention it, even though she felt weak from hunger. How could she be hungry after what had just happened?

'What do *you* think?' she whispered to her brother, partly to get her mind off the hunger.

'Ayeeyo's right, we should leave,' Roble whispered

back. A bruise was swelling on his cheek where the soldier had hit him with the gun. 'But it doesn't matter.'

'What do you mean?' Amina asked.

'She also says that if Allah wills something, it doesn't matter where you are, you'll go to meet your fate.' His shoulders slumped. 'If that's true, what's the point of leaving?'

Amina didn't know what to say. Her stomach hurt. She didn't want to leave. What if they never saw Aabbe again?

'But how can we possibly leave Somalia?' Hooyo suddenly exclaimed, jumping up, her loud frustration breaking through their whispered conversation. 'What about the baby?'

'That's exactly why we *should* leave,' Ayeeyo argued. 'Do you want the baby to be born into this?'

'No!' Hooyo said. 'But what if Samatar escapes and comes back? We would be gone. How would he ever find us?'

'We could leave a message with the neighbours,' Roble said. 'We could tell them where we plan to go and if Aabbe returns, they could let him know. Anyway, there's only one choice, right? If we go, we'll go to Kenya.'

'You're a nurse, Khadija,' Ayeeyo said. 'They need nurses everywhere. We don't have to go to Kenya. We can go to Norway or Canada or – Australia.'

Hooyo put a hand to her forehead suddenly, as if she were about to faint. Roble stood swiftly and strode to where she was, placing his arm on her shoulder. She sat down in a nearby chair, gripping his hand so hard the wrinkles on her knuckles became white lines.

'Oh, what does it matter?' she said. 'He's gone and we don't know where to look for him.'

Amina stood then and joined Roble at her mother's elbow. She knelt down in front of the chair. 'Hooyo,' she said. 'The neighbours could help us. They might know something that could help us find Aabbe.'

'It's true,' Roble agreed. 'Remember when Omar Ahmed disappeared? His family was able to find him by talking to people at Bakaara Market.'

But Hooyo said no. 'Stay near me tonight,' she murmured, reaching out. Her soft fingers wrapped around Amina's and held them tight, suffocating the itch Amina suddenly felt – the desire to go out and draw something. 'I couldn't bear to lose the two of you as well as Aabbe, all in one day.'

'What about tomorrow, Hooyo?' Roble asked.

'If we've heard nothing by tomorrow afternoon,' Hooyo said, 'then the two of you may go out and see if anybody has heard something. We will try to reach your uncle Ahmed on his phone. If he doesn't answer by tomorrow, you may go to his house. Perhaps he'll know something that will help us.'

She put her face in her hands and began to weep. It was a hopeless sound that filled the room.

A tear rolled down Amina's cheek and she quickly wiped it away.

As soon as possible, she fled upstairs. She stood with one hand on the crumbling wall and looked at the waves rollicking in the distance. Night had fallen and the last rays of red and pink light shot across the quickly darkening sky.

It was selfish but she wished Hooyo was offering *her* comfort instead of the other way around. It was true Hooyo had lost her husband – and she was expecting a baby – but Amina had lost her father. Which was worse?

She felt hollowed out of anything good and right, a deep dread skulking within. The loneliness gathered and bunched inside, a hard stone. One or two lights twinkled in the vast darkness.

She didn't want to leave.

She didn't want to stay.

She was so very afraid that she would never see Aabbe again.

She startled at a noise from behind, but it was just Roble, climbing the stairs. He kept to the edges – avoiding the danger of the floor caving in – and joined her by the wall.

She was grateful that he didn't speak but he smiled at her, gently and sadly. They stood together, watching the city – the only place they had ever known – until Amina felt the hard knot inside her begin to lessen. At least she had Roble.

◆▅◆

As usual, Amina slept with Ayeeyo in her bedroom, sharing the joodari.

Ayeeyo was a restless sleeper, moaning, sighing, even angry sometimes. She had flung her arms out and hit Amina in the face more than once. One time, she screamed, long and low, and continued screaming until Amina shook her awake.

She often talked in her sleep. Once Amina had heard her talking to her grandfather, Awoowe. 'Everything's gone now,' Ayeeyo said, and Amina wondered what she was talking about.

Tonight, Ayeeyo was silent and still. Amina lay beside her, staring up at the ceiling, listening to make sure Ayeeyo was still breathing. She kept still too so she wouldn't disturb her, but she wondered how Ayeeyo could possibly be asleep. They had gone to bed without breaking the Ramadan fast and Amina's stomach hurt from hunger. She grabbed her stomach muscles, hoping to staunch the pain, a deep weariness in her chest.

Everything seemed worse at night – scarier, more hopeless. During the day, it was possible to pretend that things weren't so bad, but at night, the constant *pop pop pop* of gunfire reminded Amina that Somalia was in the middle of a war that had been going on for a very long time.

Aabbe used to joke that gunfire was Mogadishu's lullaby. He said he no longer knew how to sleep without the chatter of machine guns echoing in the streets.

'I do not understand how it has all come to this,' Ayeeyo said, suddenly, her voice breaking the heavy silence.

Amina turned on her side, only to find her grandmother's dark eyes fixed on her.

'Somalia was once the jewel of East Africa,' she added. 'People called us the pearl of the Indian Ocean.

It has taken my husband and now my youngest son.'

'Aabbe will be all right,' Amina said. She could imagine no other possibility. If she stepped anywhere near the thought that he might not return, she knew she would fall into a fathomless abyss. She had to stay strong for Hooyo and for Aabbe and even for Roble, who was already brave but would need her to be brave with him.

'Who else will it take before this is over?' Ayeeyo's voice was relentless.

'Nobody,' Amina said. 'There is only me and Roble and Hooyo left and we go nowhere. We will be safe here, with you.' She knew that staying home didn't mean they were safe – after all, the second storey was proof of the house's vulnerabilities. And, of course, somebody had to leave every day to buy food and other necessities. And there was school and dugsi. But she wanted to stop the onslaught of Ayeeyo's hopelessness.

Ayeeyo sighed. 'How did al-Shabaab trick our men into thinking it is Allah's will that they kill each other? Why do they now believe the way of Islam is war and hate?'

Amina had no answer. Her eyes burned like she'd walked through a sandstorm, like tiny particles of rock were grinding against her eyeballs.

'It will be up to the young ones – you and Roble and your friends – to set things right,' Ayeeyo said. 'We older ones have made such a mess of our world.'

After a while, Ayeeyo must have thought Amina was asleep. She turned away and began to cry silently, her back shaking gently.

Amina didn't know what to do. She gripped the blanket tight and screwed her eyes shut, keeping perfectly still, stifling her own tears with her pillow.

◆▬◆

Hooyo shook Amina and Ayeeyo awake. Half-asleep, Amina splashed water on her face, hands and feet in the darkness, then joined the family in the alcove for Fajr prayers, offered just before sunrise, as the world first began to get light. 'Allah is the greatest,' she murmured. She tried to concentrate on the words but her mind was on her father and the meal they hadn't eaten last night.

She was starving.

After prayers, she shuffled into the kitchen. Suhuur, the morning meal during Ramadan, had to be eaten before the sun rose. Nobody mentioned Aabbe. Amina wished they would, but then she was glad they didn't. She didn't know what she wanted – except to rewind the clock.

They sat at the kitchen table, staring blankly at the fireplace where they cooked while Hooyo reheated the burnt food from the night before and dished it out. Soot from the cooking fires stained the walls and the ceiling above them. Amina found it easier to rest her eyes on the stains than on her family members.

Everything felt wrong. A dull ache burrowed itself in the pit of Amina's stomach. She wanted to cry but knew she mustn't.

She sopped the maraq up with the flat canjeero bread until there was nothing left, then gulped down a bowl of soor, the corn meal plain but filling. She drank two glasses of water and then a third, even though it made her feel full to bursting and she had to force it down. She hated getting thirsty during the long Ramadan days and having to wait until the sun set before she could drink again.

After, she waited her turn to use the toilet, near the stairs at the back of the house. Hooyo and Ayeeyo could be agonisingly slow in there. Hooyo had once explained to Amina that it was because they had both been circumcised when they were young and this had created problems. Because she was a nurse, Hooyo had decided that Amina would not undergo the surgical procedure. 'It isn't demanded by the Quran and Sunnah,' she had told Amina. 'It's our culture that demands it. But culture can be wrong.'

Amina wasn't sure what she thought about it. Like her artwork, it was yet another thing that made her different from the other girls at school, another thing that she had to keep hidden. She hoped it wouldn't create problems when it was time to get married. Somali men wouldn't want to marry a woman if she hadn't undergone the ritual. For now, she refused to mention it to anybody and hoped her parents, and Roble, kept quiet as well.

The family assembled in the front room as the sun's early morning rays broke through the window and flooded the room with bright light. Amina felt her heart lift. Surely they would find Aabbe today. They would talk or bribe their way out of the problem – even though nobody was sure who to talk to and they didn't have much money for bribes – and he would come home to them. Then life could go back to normal.

'Hooyo?' Roble stood in front of their mother.

Hooyo was looking out the window. When she turned around to face Roble, Amina caught a glimpse of her worried eyes. She looked old and tired.

Amina's hopes evaporated.

'Should we call Adeer?' Roble asked.

Hooyo shook her head. 'I've already tried calling Ahmed several times. There's no answer.'

Amina tried to remember the last time they had seen or heard from Aabbe's brother. It had been months. He lived all the way across the city.

They couldn't be sure Ahmed was alive or that he was still in Mogadishu. He had talked about leaving with his wife and children the last time the family had gathered together. It was likely that by now they had fled and were refugees in Kenya or Ethiopia.

'Then I will go and see if he's there,' Roble said. 'I will also ask around on the street to see if anybody knows anything.'

Hooyo nodded her assent and Amina leapt up. 'Can I go too, Hooyo?'

It looked as though Hooyo was about to say no but she paused. 'The boy will be safer if she goes,' Ayeeyo said.

'I'd like her to come,' Roble said. His voice was strong – nobody would ever accuse him of being a coward – but it was also quiet. He rarely expressed his desires so clearly.

'Yes, you may go,' Hooyo said at last.

Amina was already winding the scarf around her head and following Roble out the door. How could Hooyo and Ayeeyo stay hidden indoors when Aabbe was out there somewhere?

'We won't be stopping so you can draw,' Roble warned as they stepped out of the gate.

Amina automatically looked in each direction, scanning the horizon for possible signs of danger. Everything looked absurdly normal.

'I can't believe you think I would want to draw when Aabbe's—' Amina choked back the word. *Missing*. In truth, the itch was back. She would pretend it didn't exist, for now. But when she had the time, she would plaster the city with messages about her missing father. Nobody would be able to forget who he was. She would draw his face on every blank wall until somebody could help her, until she found him.

She followed Roble down the street. They cut through an alley. They climbed over a large pile of asphalt and dirt where a grenade had exploded, leaving a ditch in the middle of the road. Amina slipped on the way down, scattering pebbles, which ricocheted off the walls nearby and echoed, sharp and sudden, like a series of gunshots. *Rat-a-tat-tat-tat*.

The sound made Roble wince. 'Careful,' he said.

'I *know*,' Amina said. She hated it when he made her feel like she was in his way. And yet she *did* get in his way, she knew it. She couldn't glide, silent and quick, the way so many Somali women seemed to do, keeping themselves away from trouble. She *was* trouble, from the tips of her itchy fingers all the way down to her toes.

'I just don't want you to sprain an ankle or break your leg,' he explained and his voice was gentler.

Amina felt guilty for thinking the worst of him. 'I won't,' she promised. Then, 'Do you think Aabbe is all right?'

Roble sighed. 'I hope so.'

'Roble!' It was Keinan, shouting as he ran towards them, forgetting the rule they kept whenever they were on the streets: to be as silent as possible and not call attention to the fact that they were there. 'Roble!'

'Keinan! Hush, man! What are you trying to do? Get us killed?' Roble looked nervously this way and that.

'What are you talking about? You know I'm immortal.' He grinned then leaned over, his hands on his knees, head down, panting a little.

'We don't have time for your jokes,' Roble said. 'We're on the way to our uncle's house.'

'I've been on the watch all morning, waiting until you came out. I was afraid I might miss you.' He glanced up and gave Amina a quick smile.

Pleasure ploughed through her chest, as sharp and sudden as the noise of the pebbles that had, a few seconds before, riddled her heart with fear.

'We can't stop,' Roble said.

'I'll go with you,' Keinan said.

'No, you should go home,' Roble said. 'It's too dangerous to be seen with us.'

Amina wondered why Roble wasn't being forthright

with his best friend. 'Some men came and dragged Aabbe away from the house last night,' she blurted.

Keinan's face fell. 'I know. I heard,' he said.

Roble grabbed his friend's arm. 'Are people talking about it? What have you heard?' he asked.

Keinan's self-assurance dissipated like water sinking into the sand. 'My father,' he stuttered. 'He came home yesterday talking about it. I came by your house and rattled the gate but nobody answered.'

The look on Roble's face was anything but friendly and his voice was fierce as he asked, 'Did your father have something to do with Aabbe's arrest?'

'Why are you accusing my father?' Keinan's face flushed in anger. 'He's a good man,' he said.

'Would a good man betray his neighbour and friend?' Roble's voice was very, very quiet.

'Don't talk about betrayal to me,' Keinan said. 'He's helped your whole family for years! Your father would be *nothing* without him.'

Amina drew in a sharp breath. *Had Keinan really said that?*

'Oh, you think your family is so special, so wonderful, and mine is nothing?' Roble spat on the ground.

A man appeared on a rickety balcony nearby and stared down at them. 'What are you boys doing?' he called. 'You should go home before you get in trouble.'

'Stop arguing,' Amina shrieked, shaking her hands.

They ignored her. She felt her chest sink as they continued to shout at each other.

'I didn't say your family *is* nothing,' Keinan yelled.

'I said you have nothing unless we give it to you.'

'Nothing? We have nothing unless you give it to us?' Roble hopped up and down. His hands balled into hard fists at his sides.

'Why do you think Samatar Khalids are so popular? Why do you think they sell so well? My father is his best salesman. His *only* salesman.'

'You say we would have nothing without your father,' Amina said. 'But your father would have nothing if he didn't have Aabbe's paintings to sell.'

'Oh, please. Your father's artwork is a small drop in the ocean of business dealings my father is involved in. So don't accuse him of selling your father out just because your father got into trouble—'

Roble jabbed Keinan quickly. In the mouth. Like a snake striking.

Keinan jerked away. His mouth dripped blood.

Amina blinked, startled. She focused on the drops of bright red blood puddling on the dirt. Suddenly the two boys were rolling on the ground, grappling. Their arms were hooked in vice grips around each other's torsos. Keinan gained the upper hand. He ground Roble's face into the asphalt. Then Roble flipped Keinan over. He had Keinan in a headlock. He used a closed fist to pound him. Keinan yelped, short, high yips, like a dog.

Amina bounced around them, shrieking, 'Stop it, stop it, stop it!'

They heaved apart, gazing at each other for a moment. Then Keinan lunged and the boys tumbled back to the ground.

Amina reached into the fray and slapped Keinan's cheek as hard as she could.

Keinan glanced up and dropped his hands, pulling away from Roble. He was breathing hard, in short gasps. 'Sorry,' he muttered. 'I'm sorry. I—I don't know what I'm doing.'

Roble lay still for a few seconds as though he were exhausted. Then he rolled over, crouched on his knees, sprang up, and started running away. He dripped blood all the way down the street.

Amina shot a terrified look at Keinan and started to follow her brother.

'Hey!' Keinan shouted. 'Roble, I'm sorry. Come back!'

Roble had reached the end of the alley. He glanced over his shoulder, then jerked his head forwards again as a jeep screeched to a stop just in front of him. He veered to avoid it but a soldier with a red-and-white chequered keffiyeh wrapped around his hair and face jumped off. Only his eyes were visible. Al-Shabaab. He grabbed Roble around the neck, dragging him back towards the jeep and hustling him inside. Another soldier held the butt of an AK-47 against Roble's neck, shoving him down to the floor of the jeep with his foot.

Amina's chest felt like it was caving in as Roble disappeared from view. She started moving towards the jeep, but Keinan pulled her into a crouching position behind a large chunk of asphalt that stuck straight up from the ground.

'Keep your head down,' he hissed.

'But Roble—' she whispered.

'Right now, we have to save ourselves,' he whispered back.

She tried to stand. She wanted to see what was going on.

'Amina!' he cried. 'Al-Shabaab can't see us together – a boy and a girl? We aren't related. We aren't even cousins!' Drops of sweat glistened on his upper lip. He was still breathing heavily from the fight. The anger had died in his eyes and now he just looked scared and worried, slightly soiled from the fist fight. 'They'll kill us.'

Slowly, she sank down beside him. He was right. 'What will they do to Roble?' she asked.

'If he's smart, he'll keep his mouth shut and they'll make him into a soldier,' Keinan said. 'If he's not…'

Amina watched the jeep through a crack in the slab of asphalt, ignoring the boy beside her. The soldiers inside the jeep craned their necks, looking for any movement nearby. She stayed perfectly still.

Their guns were as long as the men were tall and each wore strands of bullets wrapped around their waists, draped over their necks and dangling down their chest. *Why did one soldier need so many bullets?* Amina wondered.

Roble had managed to raise himself from the floor of the jeep. His eyes scanned the alleyway as though he were looking for Amina and Keinan.

A soldier hit his already bruised face with the butt of the gun and Roble keeled backwards, disappearing from sight.

The jeep jolted as it started then shuddered away, taking Roble with it.

Chapter 6

Amina did not set foot outside of the house or the yard for several seemingly endless days.

Nobody came to visit, except for a woman down the street who had heard something of their troubles and brought them a box of ripe bananas.

In between prayer times, Amina wrote poetry in her head, reciting it constantly. It kept her sane, and prevented her from screaming at her mother and grandmother. Her agitated fingers tapped a restless rhythm across her thighs, in beat with the words scrolling through her head.

I remember when battles raged in my neighbourhood
and we couldn't leave the house for days.
We crouched on the floor as bullets flew overhead.
I must have been hungry but I don't remember
     wanting food.
I only wanted the war to end.
I still want the war to end.

The war is not the story I want to tell. No.
I want to tell another story, one without the bullets and
  hand grenades.
I want to tell the story of my mother's pregnancy
and the birth of a healthy, happy baby girl,
innocent,
fresh and new
like the beginning of the world.

She memorised the words so that when she found the right wall, she would be able to paint them quickly, before anybody came.

And then she started another poem.

◆▰◆

By Saturday morning, Hooyo had cooked every last morsel of food in the house. They had eaten the last cup of rice and the last bruised banana and they had only a little oil left. As they sat in the front room, she said, 'One of us must go and buy food. We have nothing left to eat.'

'I'll go,' Amina had replied automatically. She didn't want to go but it had to be her. Ayeeyo and Hooyo didn't leave the house. Besides, Ayeeyo suffered from arthritis and Hooyo was almost seven months pregnant. How could either of them run if they needed to escape danger?

But even though she was the only logical choice, Amina also *wanted* to go. She needed to escape the four walls and see what was happening on the outside. There was nothing they could do for Aabbe or Roble as long as they stayed inside. The last few days, she had felt her father and her brother slipping from her grasp as no new information came their way.

And the itch was becoming unbearable. With Aabbe gone, she could raid his supplies with impunity and not even feel guilty. Of course, she would leave all his best supplies untouched – but she could use his glue, charcoal, chalk and some water-based paints.

She had used a couple of the blank canvases stacked on the floor to create some drawings but that wasn't really what she wanted to do. To tell the truth, she had come to love the adrenalin of creating art out in the open, where it was dangerous and even haram, at least in the eyes of some Muslims.

Hooyo sighed. 'Perhaps if you go only as far as Keinan's house, his mother will sell you some food. She has both a husband and a son who can shop for her whenever she needs.'

'Yes,' Ayeeyo said. 'That way you don't have to travel so far.'

'Perhaps,' Amina mumbled, knowing she would never go to Keinan's house for help.

Although she wasn't sure why, she hadn't told her mother about how Keinan and Roble had fought in the street just before Roble was taken or of Roble's suspicions that the family was somehow connected to al-Shabaab and was behind Aabbe's abduction, suspicions which she now knew were true: Keinan had practically admitted his family's guilt. The walk home had been virtually silent, punctured by occasional defensive outbursts from Keinan that sounded only vaguely apologetic. 'It's just that my father is good at business,' he said. 'He makes money, that's what he does. He sells things…he knows everybody…he…' His voice drifted off.

He sells things, Amina thought. *And people? Does he sell people too? Did he sell my father?*

'I'm not my father,' Keinan said, too, in a burst of anger.

It was absurd for him to say that, Amina thought. *Of course he wasn't his father. And yet he* was. *How could she separate Keinan from his father or his father's guilt? It was impossible.*

'I'm sorry,' he added.

Sorry for what? Amina had wondered. Sorry for your father's actions? Sorry that because of you, Roble has been taken by al-Shabaab?

She could barely look at him, she was so angry. So she had ignored him until they reached her gate, when she looked him in the eye and said, '*Goodbye,* Keinan.'

Her dismissal had angered him. She had listened to the furious sound of his feet as he stomped off in the direction of his house.

So why hadn't she told Hooyo the story while she was still angry? Even though she was angry, she must have been protecting Keinan…She liked him *that* much, she realised.

Now the anger was gone and she wished that she had met him halfway. She could have said, *I know you didn't mean to hurt Roble and I know you had nothing to do*

with Aabbe's disappearance, no matter what your father did.
She missed Keinan and his boasting. She still liked him,
despite everything.

Hooyo continued, with a knowing look, 'And besides,
that family has plenty of money. They have robbed us
blind, with what they charge for Samatar's paintings
at the market and what they turn around and pay us.
Somalis in America have lots of money and they are the
ones buying Samatar's work.'

Amina felt a stab of renewed anger at Keinan's
family, for growing rich on Aabbe's paintings and then
handing him over to the people who wanted to kill him,
all because it meant more money in their pockets.

'I always told Roble not to hang around that boy,'
Hooyo said.

Why was Hooyo acting like things had been different?
She used to sit in the front room and laugh at the boys'
antics. She would listen to Keinan's boasting and say, 'You
are too much, son.' *Son.* She had always called him son.

Amina's anger was a missile seeking heat and Hooyo
was the hottest thing around. 'Hooyo,' she said. 'You
always liked Keinan. Don't pretend.'

Hooyo raised her eyebrows. Her voice crackled with
laughter. 'Is this my own daughter, contradicting me?'

'Yes,' Amina said, rage in her voice.

'Oh! You are right,' she said, and she sounded
weary. 'I had a weakness for that boy. But now I see I
was wrong. I should have warned Roble to stay away
from the family. I should have told Aabbe we could find
somebody else to sell his paintings.'

'Abdullahi Hassan is playing a dangerous game,' Amina said. 'I'm sure Aabbe's paintings aren't the only thing he sells that al-Shabaab considers haram, and yet he is aligning himself with al-Shabaab.'

'It is dangerous,' Ayeeyo agreed. 'And he will pay for it some day, perhaps with his life. You'll see.'

'Why does Aabbe sell his paintings at Bakaara Market?' Amina asked, suddenly curious. 'Why doesn't he sell them in a gallery, like Ibrahim?'

Amina had accompanied Aabbe to his colleague's gallery openings. Ibrahim created abstract designs, constructed from the remnants of broken tiles. They were beautifully rendered pieces of art, seemingly haphazard at first glance but actually deliberate and careful on closer inspection. His work had inspired Amina to create her first piece, the mosaic constructed from broken glass and stones, as well as subsequent pieces made from discarded cloth or tiles.

Hooyo's hands, which had been busy plaiting Amina's hair, suddenly stilled. 'We never told you why?'

Amina shook her head. 'I knew there was a problem but not what the problem was.'

Hooyo didn't answer immediately. Her hands were rough as she twisted Amina's hair.

'His paintings were already banned by the Islamic Courts Union a few years ago when they were in power,' Ayeeyo said. 'Too political, they said. And, of course, he always painted people and animals and they said that was un-Islamic. That's why he quit his job at the university – it made him a target. Al-Shabaab is just carrying on with the judgement of the courts.'

So Aabbe had made himself a target with his work.

'He always had to criticise everything and everybody.' An undercurrent of frustration surged in Hooyo's words.

'You mean that he was an artist,' Amina said. 'He said what he needed to say. He didn't have a choice.'

'I mean that he couldn't just paint a pretty picture to make some money,' Hooyo snapped. 'He always had to make a statement, no matter what it cost us.' She stood abruptly and exited, leaving Amina alone with Ayeeyo.

Amina felt desolate. Even Ibrahim's works, which might seem like little more than pretty pieces of art, sent a definitive message about what he believed in and hoped for – the idea that in this world order could emerge out of chaos. Wasn't that also political? Perhaps Aabbe's work was just more blatantly political.

'I *like* Aabbe's work,' she said.

Ayeeyo smoothed Amina's hair, her gnarled hands slow and gentle. 'So does your mother,' she said. 'She's just hurting. You must be very kind to her now.'

Hearing the reminder made Amina grumpy. 'I'm always kind to Hooyo,' she said.

'Even kinder than usual,' Ayeeyo amended.

Ayeeyo was asking a lot. Wasn't Hooyo the mother? Wasn't she, Amina, the child? Hooyo had lost a husband and a son, but Amina had lost her father and her brother. She was the one who now had to face the world for the family – and the world was not a safe place. If somebody needed to be kind, why did it have to be Amina? Why shouldn't it be Hooyo?

'Ibrahim is no longer exhibiting in galleries,' Ayeeyo said. 'It is too dangerous even for him.'

'I see,' Amina said. She had known her own work was dangerous but now she truly realised it could bring her death. Would that stop her? She wasn't sure. That itch was there…she could feel it even now.

'Go now, my little butterfly, and buy some food for us to cook.' Ayeeyo prodded Amina.

Shillings in hand, Amina wrapped a bright gold scarf around her head. She slipped out the door, hoping Hooyo would get some rest while she was gone.

She stole into Aabbe's studio and grabbed a piece of charcoal. Beyond the poem she had been composing, she had been thinking about what she would draw or write next and, though it was still amorphous in her mind, perhaps she could pull a piece together when she was actually facing a blank wall and had a few spare moments to herself.

The streets were surprisingly crowded. Men stood under trees, chewing khat and chatting, spitting globs of green onto the dirt. Women walked down the broken footpaths, dressed in long, colourful jalabeeb, reds and oranges and pinks and purples, only their hands and faces visible. They carried baskets of vegetables and pasta, flashing white teeth as they spoke to each other. Children buzzed about beside them, playing tag, dashing across the street, laughing loudly.

One of the mothers shouted suddenly and the

children ran, scattering to either side of the street. They heard the rumbling of trucks coming their way. Younger children clung to their mothers' hands.

A caravan of trucks tried to drive down the street, but people surrounded it. Street children were swarming over each truck, and men were jostling each other with sticks as the caravan inched its way through the crowd. Each truck had a soldier standing in or hanging off the back end, his finger idle on an AK-47. One of them pointed his gun into the crowd and shot, scattering people so that the convoy could move more swiftly down the street.

Amina ducked into an abandoned building and waited, breathing hard, until the caravan passed. Then she stepped outside again, only to discover another convoy of trucks headed her way.

She escaped into her hiding place again and sat with her back against the wall, listening to the clamour of trucks and soldiers shouting and the occasional loud *pffft-pfft-pffffffft* as they shot guns into the air. One of them shot the building she was in and she heard the loud *ping* echo throughout the four walls as the bullet ricocheted and shattered the last remaining glass window.

She crouched down and quickly drew a picture of her father, scribbling a message beneath: *Samatar Khalid, taken from his home in Mogadishu.*

She had decided she would draw his picture everywhere, whenever she got a chance. She felt compelled to make sure nobody forgot who he was. Thousands of other men and women in Mogadishu had disappeared – people who had never come home to their families because they had been abducted or killed. She couldn't draw all of them – there were too many, and she didn't know most of them – but she could pay tribute by allowing her father's picture to stand in for all of them.

Quickly, she added the phrase 'one of many' to her message.

She wondered if she should eliminate her usual signature A and the Somali star. Recognition was dangerous. But in the end, she signed her work anyway.

◆▰◆

The gunfire sounded further away, so she risked emerging from the building and peeking around the corner of the wall to the street. She could just see the last of the trucks in the convoy disappearing in the distance.

Amina dashed one block to the left and another to the right, glancing both ways as she reached the neighbourhood market. It was empty. The men and women normally selling everything she needed were gone. They had escaped indoors or had joined the convoy headed out of the city.

Amina hesitated. Should she continue looking for food, even begging Keinan's mother to help them? Or should she go home?

Shots rang in the street behind her and suddenly the decision was made. Her breath came in short, jagged gasps as she hurtled down the street and through the gate, slamming it shut behind her.

Amina closed the front door and undid her scarf with trembling fingers. She was glad she had made the decision to come home, even though her stomach was already growling.

She wondered what she could tell Hooyo and Ayeeyo that would make them feel better about going hungry tonight. Especially Hooyo. She must be ravenous because of the baby.

◆▸■◂◆

Ayeeyo grasped Amina tight. 'Alhamdulillah, thank God.'

'I'm safe, Ayeeyo,' Amina said against her chest.

Ayeeyo released her from the embrace.

'What's going on out there?' Hooyo asked.

'I don't know,' Amina said. 'Seven or eight trucks drove past, full of soldiers. Al-Shabaab. They were shooting guns into the street. I couldn't tell if they were happy or angry.'

'We heard the trucks rumbling past. I even told Ayeeyo to go upstairs and look.'

'Can you imagine me, your old grandmother, walking up those crumbling stairs?' Ayeeyo shook her head. 'No! We went outside instead and peeked through a crack in the wall.'

'We could hardly see anything,' Hooyo admitted.

'Do you think another army has taken over our neighbourhood?' Amina asked.

Hooyo shivered. 'We must just pray for good news.'

Amina went and stood beside her mother. 'You should rest,' she said to Hooyo. 'Ayeeyo and I will look again to see if we can find something, anything, to eat.'

Hooyo shook her head. 'It's no use,' she said. 'The kitchen is empty. There is nothing.'

'Let us determine that,' Amina said.

Amina looked at her grandmother expectantly, as though Ayeeyo might have some answers. But her grandmother simply had tears in her eyes.

'We have nothing to eat?'

Ayeeyo shook her head. 'Nothing.'

Amina walked outside. She searched Aabbe's studio. Was there any chance he had kept food in there? Even if Amina and Ayeeyo went hungry, Hooyo – and the baby – needed food. She crept inside and began a long search through canvases, tubes of paint, charcoal, paintbrushes and sheets of paper. No food anywhere.

She looked at the house and noticed that her bedroom window had shattered. A stray bullet must have hit it this afternoon, while she was gone.

The exterior of the house was a wreck. And yet tiny details had survived the mayhem and destruction of the last decade. An intricate design wrapped around the entire house in layered strips of concrete. The curved pane of blue glass was still intact and reflected blue light inside the alcove where they prayed. Bits of beauty remained, despite the chaos.

Amina gathered up the clear glass quickly, placing it in a bucket, which she put in Aabbe's studio. She could use it later for a project.

She went to the house, closing the door carefully behind her. Ayeeyo was watching.

Amina shook her head in response to the unasked question. 'Aabbe didn't have food in his studio.'

Ayeeyo nodded. 'Your mother is especially tired,'

she said. 'I sent her to bed. We will find food tomorrow.'

Amina went to her parents' room and sat down beside their joodari. Hooyo was pale and tired. She lay in a foetal position on the mat, hugging her belly, and looked at Amina with large, fearful eyes.

An unnamed fear slammed against Amina and left her breathless. 'What's wrong, Hooyo?'

Hooyo was quiet for a time.

'What's wrong?' Amina asked again, prodding her mother.

'I'm bleeding,' Hooyo admitted.

'No!' Aabbe. Roble. Not Hooyo. She couldn't lose Hooyo, too. Or the baby... The baby couldn't come yet. Would Hooyo want to have the baby here, at home? And how were Amina and Ayeeyo supposed to deliver a baby? Even if they knew what to do, it was too early. The baby would not survive, not unless they were in the best hospital in the world.

'Hooyo,' she said. Her hand hovered over Hooyo's belly but she dared not touch her. She had no idea what her mother needed or wanted.

They looked at each other and Hooyo sighed. She grabbed Amina's hand and held it to her chest. Amina felt the soft *thump-thump-thumping* of her mother's heart.

Hooyo's eyes drooped shut and Amina's hand drifted lower, towards her belly. She waited, hoping with all her heart that she would feel the tiny butterfly flutter that said the baby was moving, dancing, laughing inside the womb. A girl. Amina hoped it was a little girl, a little sister. She needed another ally.

But like the food she had searched for earlier, there was nothing. Absolute stillness, as if the baby were hiding in a dark corner of Hooyo's womb.

Amina sat there as the afternoon sun filtered in the window, her hand on her mother's belly. In the front room, Ayeeyo shuffled around, readying herself for Maghrib prayers, offered after sunset.

Amina did not move. Dusk turned to darkness and she sat there in silence, listening to the sound of her mother breathing.

She stayed there until she heard Ayeeyo hobbling around again in the front room, now for Isha prayers, offered just before bed. She stood and joined her grandmother in the alcove. Ablutions first, then kneeling on the sijaayad, facing towards Mecca. Her heart was full and her prayers reflected it – for Aabbe, for Hooyo, for Roble. For Ayeeyo and for herself, as well.

Neither Amina nor Ayeeyo went to bed when they were done. Gunshots intermittently shattered the night's stillness. Amina sat beside her mother in her parents' bedroom, a prayer on her lips, feeling the desperation, hoping that in the morning, Hooyo would tell her that everything was well. Every once in a while, she climbed the stairs that led to the second floor, where she could look out and watch orange flares lighting the night all around her. Gun battles, everywhere she could see.

Where were Aabbe and Roble? Were they in the middle of all of this?

She breathed until the sadness had dissipated. She longed for the morning.

Chapter 7

Amina woke – huddled beside Hooyo's joodari, cramped and cold. The sounds of gun battles that had raged throughout the night were replaced by people's startled shouts as they ran past the house.

Hooyo's eyes were open. She stared at the wall and didn't move until Amina placed a gentle hand on her arm. Then she roused herself, bedclothes rustling, shaking Amina's hand off.

'How are you?' Amina wanted to be more direct – to ask if her mother was still bleeding. She didn't dare. She hoped Hooyo would get the hint.

Hooyo ignored her and Amina decided that her mother's silence meant yes to her unasked question.

'Let me help you,' she said, holding out an arm so that Hooyo could lean on her and walk to the toilet.

Hooyo disregarded her arm, hobbling slowly from the bed to the toilet by herself.

Amina waited while her mother performed her morning rituals and then followed her back to bed.

Hooyo was too ill to join them for prayers so Amina and Ayeeyo prayed alone. Amina went through the motions but she knew she was only reciting, just repeating the words after her grandmother. She felt listless and dull. She was hungry but knew there would be no food after prayers – not because it was Ramadan and they were late to prayer this morning but because she had failed to find food the day before.

The day was long. Amina stood at the open gate and watched men and women scurrying about, blinking in the bright sun like rats who have come to the surface after a long time in the dark. Something big had happened and it would be easy to find out what it was – all she had to do was ask somebody who was walking past – but she didn't feel like asking.

She closed the gate and went back to the house.

There was no change in Hooyo's condition, though she did sit up in the afternoon, tired and pale, eyes huge in her face. Ayeeyo brought her tea, breaking the Ramadan fast. 'You must have something to eat or drink, daughter,' she said. 'For the baby. You're a good Muslim but you need to break the fast. You must agree.'

Amina sat on the edge of Hooyo and Aabbe's joodari while Hooyo sipped the tea. She wanted to reach out and hold her mother's hand but they'd never had that kind of easy relationship. She wished Roble were here.

Everything in her life was slipping away – first Aabbe, then Roble, then Keinan and now Hooyo and the baby. What could she do to save her mother and her unborn brother or sister? A sister. It was going to be a sister.

It had to be – she was sure of it. Amina sent a prayer heavenward for her unborn sister.

Tea was all they had for the evening meal when Amina and Ayeeyo went to break the Ramadan fast. They each drank four cups to hold back the hunger pains for a few hours. Though they had no milk, at least it was sweet with a touch of cinnamon.

In bed, Amina's belly hurt so badly she had to grip her sides to try to stop the pain.

◆▬◆

By Monday, the streets seemed quieter.

Amina took some money, covered her head and arms, and went outside. At the market, the stalls were mostly empty. Instead, people stood in small groups, sharing rumours, spreading the news, explaining what they knew or had heard or had seen. That was the way of Mogadishu. Everybody knew everybody else's business. If something happened in one hour, you could be sure the news would have reached the other end of the city by the next.

Amina stood beside one group of women that she recognised, though not by name. She had seen them around the neighbourhood occasionally when she went to and from school or joined Roble on an errand.

'What's happening, eeddo?' she politely asked the woman who stood next to her.

'You haven't heard?' she replied. She was an older woman, dressed conservatively in a dark blue jalbaab with a khimar pulled low over her forehead and high over her mouth. Soft wrinkles lined the skin around her eyes.

Amina's mouth was dry and there was a bitter taste on the tip of the tongue. No, she hadn't heard. She said nothing and waited for the woman to tell her.

'Al-Shabaab fled Mogadishu on Saturday,' the woman said. She looked at Amina as if judging what her reaction would be.

'Isn't that good news?' Amina said. At the same time, her heart sank. Roble was with al-Shabaab. Aabbe might be too. What had happened to them? She didn't want to think about it too much.

'What does it matter?' the woman said. 'There is not enough food.'

'There will be,' Amina said, but she felt no conviction in the words. She had to say it, it had to be true...but what if it wasn't?

She left the group of gossiping women and walked four blocks north and three blocks south, staying within the boundaries of her neighbourhood, unsure what she might find if she stepped outside. With al-Shabaab gone, who knew what might have changed?

As she walked, she grew hot and damp underneath all the layers of clothes, from the combination of sun, the temperature, the lack of wind. She saw the streets filled with people and boys playing soccer in their bare feet.

Life had already changed – but the old woman was right, food was scarce. She found a woman selling vegetables, but she was aghast at the price. Still, she paid it. They needed to eat something.

On her own street, she joined another group of neighbours when she overheard a woman ask, 'Do you think al-Shabaab is gone for good?'

'We've been through this before, haven't we?' replied a woman who lived a few doors down from Amina.

The group murmured its agreement until a third woman said, 'Yes, but this time, those African Union soldiers are here. They've taken back the stadium and they say they're moving into all the neighbourhoods. That's why al-Shabaab left. If the government returns to power, maybe it'll be different this time.'

The African Union soldiers had assisted Somalia's government before in its attempts to regain control of the city. Amina wondered if it would be different this time. Would Somalis ever succeed in finding peace and a stable government?

From the corner of her eyes, Amina noticed that Keinan's gate was opening. She shifted so that she could see better and pretended to be absorbed in what the woman was saying.

Keinan walked through the gate and looked at the women standing a few metres away. His presence was a tight squeeze around her heart. It embarrassed and alarmed her, this flood of happiness, all because she saw the boy whose family had betrayed her father. Where was the anger? A trickle of sweat dripped down her neck and dribbled down her back.

'I hope so,' the first woman said. 'I'm tired of war. It's all we can remember.' She pointed at Amina. 'This girl has never known anything but war. Think of that!'

Even as they all stared at her, Amina still felt Keinan's eyes on her. She ignored him, as she was supposed to do when elders were present. It hurts though. She wanted to let him know she wasn't angry anymore. She wanted to let him know how she felt and maybe—

Keinan closed the gate and walked away.

Amina's heart dropped between her toes and suddenly she lost interest in the conversation.

'But what's the difference if your neighbourhood is controlled by a war lord or al-Shabaab or the government when you're hungry?' one of the women asked. 'I just want to feed my family.'

'It's this stupid drought,' another woman said. 'Maybe we will have peace now – but even if the government is back in power, they can't make it rain.'

Amina went into her yard and sat on the steps leading to the house. She didn't want to go into the house yet – she wanted to think for a while, and feel unhappy, without Ayeeyo asking her what was wrong. She couldn't explain about Keinan. It was too complicated. Her family would not want her pining after some boy, especially one whose family might have something to do with Aabbe's disappearance. She wasn't engaged to Keinan. She was supposed to pretend he didn't exist.

◆━━◆

The three remaining weeks of Ramadan dragged by. There was food available but, because of the drought, it was so expensive that they couldn't afford to buy much.

Ayeeyo parcelled out the money carefully, worried about how quickly it was disappearing, and for such small amounts of food. She was simply prolonging the inevitable.

Amina returned to school after the first week of Ramadan. But she found it difficult to concentrate with her growling belly.

Basra noticed that Amina had nothing to eat during the morning break and that she had eyed the mangoes hungrily, wondering aloud when they'd be ripe enough to pick. She sat next to Amina beside the mango tree and offered to share her food.

'Oh, no, thank you,' Amina said. Her pride wouldn't let her accept. 'I'm not hungry.'

'Whatever you say,' Basra replied. 'But I have more food than I can eat.'

So Amina accepted a canjeero – a sheet of flat, round bread – and half a mango. She tried to eat casually, daintily, like Basra herself, when really she wanted to rip into the food like a wild animal, juices rolling down her arms and dripping off her elbows.

'Where's Roble?' Basra asked. 'He hasn't been waiting for you after school like he used to.'

It was true, these days Amina walked to school alone – just like she went everywhere alone now. Her longed-for freedom tasted bitter in her mouth.

Amina noticed her friend's pink cheeks and hurried glance away as she asked, as though she didn't care, and she guessed what Basra's interest really meant. Still, even though Basra seemed like a kind girl, she couldn't tell the world the family's secrets. What if Roble managed to escape and come back? It would be better if nobody knew that he'd been kidnapped by al-Shabaab, that he might even be fighting for them, wherever they had fled. That was assuming, of course, that Keinan was keeping quiet about it as well.

So she mumbled something about her mother needing Roble at home.

Basra munched thoughtfully on her own piece of canjeero. 'That is too bad. School is important.'

'Yes,' Amina agreed.

'We are meeting at Filad's again today,' Basra said. 'Would you like to come?'

'I can't,' Amina said. 'I have to go home and help my mother.'

Basra's lively black eyes indicated that she knew there must be a problem at home, but she didn't ask. 'Well, if you change your mind, you are always welcome.'

Amina returned her smile, wishing with all her heart that she could go.

◆▬◆

After school, Amina skipped dugsi. She didn't think she could concentrate on lessons and homework when she was so hungry.

On the way home, she stopped at the market for a few potatoes, an onion, some tea and a little bit of sugar. She wondered how Basra's family had money enough for so much food. Maybe Basra's father was a shrewd businessman, like Keinan's father.

'It's so expensive, Ayeeyo,' Amina said when her grandmother clucked at how little she brought home.

'The drought has made everything scarce,' Ayeeyo said. 'People are desperate so they'll pay anything.'

'They say several charities flew food in for people who are hungry,' Amina said. 'But al-Shabaab set fire to it.'

'They will answer to Allah for their murderous hearts!' Ayeeyo exclaimed. 'To let people starve!'

Every day Amina bought food at the market, but it was never enough. Each night, they went to bed hungry.

Amina had noticed that Ayeeyo would put most of her portion on Hooyo's plate. If Hooyo had been herself, she would have refused it. Huddled on her bed day and night, except when she had to go to the toilet or bathe, Hooyo was unaware that Ayeeyo was giving up her food.

As much as Hooyo needed that food, what about Ayeeyo? She was old and frail. She needed it too.

'What should we do?' Amina asked one night. She'd spent the last of the money at the market that day. The meal had consisted of a small potato apiece and a cup of sweet, weak tea. Amina still felt shaky with hunger. 'We're out of money and out of food. Should we try reaching Uncle Ahmed again?'

'I have tried calling every day,' Ayeeyo said. 'The phone rings and rings and rings. Either something has happened to them or they've fled. But I have a different idea.'

After washing up, she took Amina by the hand and led her outside, down the steps, and across to Aabbe's studio. Ayeeyo opened the door and Amina followed her inside.

Ayeeyo gestured at several of the finished paintings. 'People recognise the work of Samatar Khalid,' she said. 'We must take some of these paintings to our neighbour and ask him to do what he has always done: to sell them and bring us part of the profit.'

'We can't do that.' Amina took a deep breath. 'He's the one that handed Aabbe over to the people who came and took him. Keinan told us so, the day al-Shabaab took Roble.'

Ayeeyo leaned against the wall, a spark lighting and then dying in her eyes. Anger ... and then despair.

'But if it's as you say, that people recognise Samatar Khalids, then *we* can try to sell one of his paintings,' Amina said. 'Let's go to Bakaara Market tomorrow.' She thought about how long it had been since Ayeeyo had left the house. Years. 'Or I'll go alone and see if I can find a buyer for Aabbe's work.'

'No, no,' Ayeeyo said. 'It's too dangerous. His work has been banned. What if the wrong person sees you?'

'What else are we going to do?' Amina asked. 'We have to eat. We need money.'

Ayeeyo sat down. Short and stooped, she looked lost in Aabbe's high stool, the one he had used while painting.

Amina realised, by the silence, that Ayeeyo had acquiesced to her plan. 'Don't tell Hooyo where I've gone tomorrow,' Amina said. 'She'll worry and she doesn't need that.'

'I may be old and arthritic, but I'm not useless,'

Ayeeyo said. 'How would you even find the market without me? I'll go with you and we will tell your mother the truth.'

◆▰◆

Amina had trouble sleeping. To still the thumping of her heart, she listened to the soft breathing from her grandmother and then to Ayeeyo's mumbling, her sleep-talking. These were normal night sounds.

But that evening, they failed to comfort her. She spent the entire night avoiding sleep and the dreams that stalked her when she succumbed – dreams where she was running through the city streets, pursued by a reckless army shouting strange slogans and brandishing sticks of charcoal like weapons.

Chapter 8

Early the next morning, Amina wrapped herself in several layers of cloth over her skirt and draped her entire torso with a long, maroon jalbaab and matching khimar, leaving only her face uncovered. Ayeeyo handed her one of Aabbe's smaller paintings, folded inside a long, black cloth. She fished shillings out of her pocket and told Amina she was splitting the money between them. Ayeeyo insisted that Amina carry the emergency mobile phone, so she could call Hooyo if there were problems or if they were separated.

'Do you think we'll find trouble?' Amina asked. She tucked the painting under the jalbaab.

'No, insha'Allah, God willing,' Ayeeyo murmured.

Hooyo sat up in bed to drink tea, the only thing they had for breakfast. 'Be careful,' she said. Her eyes were enormous in her shrunken face. For a second, Amina doubted her decision to go, but they needed money to buy food.

Hooyo had consulted an old tome hidden away in

the bookcase in the front room and had written down a list of herbs to buy at the market if they were successful in selling Aabbe's painting. Herbs to stop Hooyo's bleeding and stabilise her hormones: shepherd's purse, vitex, cramp bark or wild yam.

'But where will I find these herbs?' Amina asked. They weren't common herbs. 'Why would anybody have these?'

'You can find anything in Bakaara Market, if you have enough money and know the right people,' Hooyo said. 'But things can be expensive. So… don't even go looking unless there's enough money. Food is more important.'

Amina decided then that there would be enough money for the herbs Hooyo needed, no matter what. And she would find the right people.

◆■◆

The wind was singing through the palm trees when they set out, the fresh air smelling of salt from the ocean. Cumulous clouds tumbled endlessly through the bright blue sky and seagulls cried as they flew overhead. It was still early and the streets were empty except for a woman cooking over a fire in one of the abandoned houses on their street.

They stepped into the street, Ayeeyo mumbling prayers under her breath, and set off in the general direction of the market. It had been a long time since Ayeeyo had been there and nobody knew which landmarks would have survived the last twenty years of war – the gun battles, rockets and mortar shells, missiles from American drone attacks.

Though Ayeeyo said the walk would take less than an hour, it crossed so many invisible political boundaries that Amina felt like they were traversing into another world.

The last time Amina had been to the market, she had been a young girl. Then the market became a stronghold for al-Shabaab. Some people said it was the largest arms market in all of Africa. If you wanted a weapon, you could find it there. And that was what made it too dangerous. You never knew when there might be a bombing or a gunfight. Aabbe had gone only occasionally, mostly to get what he needed for his work, and he hadn't even allowed Roble to accompany him.

But the market was one of the first places that the African Union soldiers had secured earlier that summer. For a while, they said the market had been empty and lifeless. Now, it was patrolled by African Union soldiers instead of al-Shabaab. Even though the risk was still there, the market was safer than it had been.

Amina's head throbbed but she ignored it, just as she had learned to ignore the dull, constant twinge in her belly that tried to remind her she was hungry. She was gripping Aabbe's painting so hard that her fingers started to hurt. She unfurled and stretched them to reduce the pain.

Ahead, Amina could see that the gate to Keinan's house was open. As they neared it, Keinan and his father stepped out into the street, both immaculately dressed in white slacks, Keinan wearing a yellow tunic and his father a blue one. They turned right.

Amina slowed down, putting her arm out to hold Ayeeyo back as well. The last thing she wanted was to greet Keinan and pretend that everything was all right.

After a few blocks it became clear that Keinan and his father were headed the same way as Amina and her grandmother – to the market. Amina considered ducking into a side alley and finding an alternative way, but the easiest thing to do was to just follow. Keinan and his father knew the way, after all, and getting lost was a huge risk. She and Ayeeyo would keep a careful distance.

Their feet kicked up dust on the dirt roads and footpaths. Though it was early, the sun was already hot, soaking through the dark folds of Amina's jalbaab. She looked at Ayeeyo, a thin layer of dust already coating her black skirt, and wondered that she didn't feel faint.

Keinan and his father seemed determined to keep a fast pace. It was especially hard for Ayeeyo to walk that quickly but she did her best and refused to complain.

They passed a mosque. Amina's eyes absorbed the white columns and the walls' knobby spires pointing like arrows to the sky. She noted the lovely black lines engraved down the sides of the walls in elaborate patterns. It was just another small example of delicate architectural beauty that had survived the many years of war.

'Do you need to lean on my arm?' she asked when Ayeeyo finally slowed down.

'It's just so hot,' Ayeeyo puffed. She gripped Amina's arm, leaving a sweaty handprint on the jalbaab.

Amina paused as they passed an abandoned street, drawing in a breath as she observed its sere and brutal beauty: the skeletons of houses, only bearing walls left standing. One white three-storey house remained mostly intact, its upper floors charred black, one wall broken off to form a sharp spear pointing towards the sky. A car had been left to rot halfway down the street, its doors ripped off, its shell riddled with bullets.

Once or twice, Amina was afraid they had lost sight of Keinan when he and his father turned a corner. She wondered at her own audacity – to assume that they were going to the market and then to follow them as though that were true. But following them kept her from noticing the potential threats to safety that lingered on all sides. When she realised that two strangers were following discreetly ten or twenty paces behind, she sped up to Keinan and his father to close the gap between them. Surely Keinan would not let somebody harm her, just because they'd had a disagreement.

In fact, Keinan had slowed his walk the tiniest bit, making it easier for Amina to catch up. He inclined his head, as though he was looking towards his father, but when he lifted his hand to acknowledge her and then nodded his head deferentially towards Ayeeyo, her cheeks warmed and her heart fluttered. He knew they were following. And he *was* watching out for them.

She suddenly became convinced that Keinan could not have taken part in her father's betrayal. His father might have been involved, but not Keinan. She trusted him. How could she have forgotten that? How could Roble have forgotten? Keinan had always been a good friend to her brother.

Ayeeyo halted unexpectedly and Amina stumbled.

Ayeeyo turned to face the two men that had started following them. 'Shame,' she hissed. 'Shame.'

Amina's whole body went hot-cold and her forehead felt clammy. What was Ayeeyo doing?

The two men approached, staring at them, eyes hostile. Amina looked left and right. What should they do if the men attacked?

That's when she noticed that Keinan and his father had dropped back. They lingered nearby, waiting, watching.

The men's eyes shuddered left and right, taking in the surroundings – the walled compounds, the shells of former houses, the street deserted except for the four of them and Keinan and his father. Then they stalked past, barely pausing, though one turned and glanced back at them, his gaze harsh and angry.

Amina let out the breath she'd been holding. Black spots danced in front of her eyes and she paused to let the wave of nausea subside. The last thing she should do was to pass out right now.

Keinan and his father started walking again as soon as the men passed them. They all turned around a corner, disappearing from view.

Ayeeyo started trembling. She leaned heavily on Amina. 'They were trouble,' she said. 'What have we come to, that two men would mean an old woman and a young girl harm?'

'I don't know, Ayeeyo,' Amina said. Fear of strangers had always been part of her life. She had never known the world any other way. She'd only heard stories of the world as it used to be, when everybody was family, when nobody was a stranger, no matter where you were in Somalia. Sometimes they pretended it was still like that – but they knew better. 'In any case, Keinan and his father helped protect us.'

'Yes,' Ayeeyo said. 'It shows that they are not evil, even if they have done our family great damage.'

Ayeeyo was like that – always trying to see the good in people. It was one of the things Amina most liked about her.

They turned the corner. Amina expected Keinan and his father to be long gone, but they were waiting several blocks ahead. They turned left almost as soon as Amina and Ayeeyo came into view.

The other men were nowhere to be seen.

'It's so hot,' Ayeeyo complained.

'Yes,' Amina agreed. She felt like she would collapse under Ayeeyo's weight.

As they limped towards the street where Keinan had disappeared, a cacophony of bellowing voices, laughter, clucking chickens and even the bleating of a goat announced their arrival at the market.

They turned the corner and Amina stood stock-still. It felt as though she had never seen a street so full of life, though she knew she had been here before. The memory was washed away with this new assault on her senses.

The street was lined with colourful umbrellas shading the various stalls. Boxes were heaped with shoes and stacks of bright cloth. Tables were piled high with bananas and mobile phones. Other tables groaned under the weight of thick green stalks of khat.

Men and women moved slowly down the street, like small herds of camels ambling along a ravine, stopping here and there to sniff food or glance through a pile of stuff. Several men carted wheelbarrows of cement down the middle of the road, careening dangerously through people clustered in groups near stalls and shopfronts.

Amina smelled dust and roasting meat and burning fires and sweat and it made her feel faint, all of it.

Life, she thought. This is life!

And then she thought of the men trading guns in Aabbe's painting of the market. She thought of how al-Shabaab had controlled the market until just a few short months ago. It was life, but maybe it was death also.

Amina started to move towards the stalls but Ayeeyo stopped her. 'Wait. I need to rest for a moment. Did I ever tell you about coming here as a child?'

Amina shook her head no.

'My father would trade camel's milk and goat hides for whatever we needed and then we would go back out into the countryside for the rest of the year, moving from place to place. I thought the city had everything. Everything we didn't have. How I wanted to live here.'

'And now you do,' Amina said.

'And now I do,' Ayeeyo repeated. She looked sad.

Amina thought about the hard but simple life of the men and women who herded their camels through Somalia's hot arid regions, the countryside. 'I would like to live out in the middle of nowhere,' Amina said, 'if it meant escaping all of this.'

'The market?' Ayeeyo asked. 'Or the city?'

Amina wondered how she could explain. She shook her head, unable to continue. It wasn't the market or the city. It was the violence. The stress of never knowing whether she would live to see another day. Sometimes she forgot the fear, but when she remembered, it was worse than if she'd never forgotten. Because what kind of person could forget that you were living in the middle of a warzone?

'This is your city, your country,' Ayeeyo said. 'All of this – the good and the bad. We are your family. You can never leave Somalia – even if you don't live here, it's with you, wherever you go in the world.'

'I know,' Amina said. 'But sometimes I wish Aabbe and Hooyo had made a different choice.'

'You wish they had left?' Something sparked in Ayeeyo's eyes. 'Do you think your father and brother would still be here with you?'

Maybe Hooyo was right, that if everybody good left, Somalia would never be a better place – but the family had paid a hard sacrifice for that belief. Still, what if Ayeeyo was right? What if your fate was already written by Allah, no matter where you lived? Amina wasn't sure she wanted to believe that.

'I'm not sure what I think,' Amina said. 'I'm just sad.'

Ayeeyo squeezed her arm. 'Me too, my little butterfly. Me too. We cannot tell what might have been different. We can only live with what is.'

For a moment, Amina thought Ayeeyo had rallied and recovered. But talking seemed to have worn her out. Even though she was holding Amina's arm, she stumbled and then sank down to her knees on a stoop. 'You go on,' she said. 'I need more time to rest.'

A young woman sitting nearby behind a pile of bananas smiled at Ayeeyo. 'Do you want some water, eeddo?' she asked. Ayeeyo gratefully accepted the warm water in a cracked plastic cup. The woman gestured towards a chair and Ayeeyo sank into it, heaving a sigh.

'Do you need anything?' The woman pointed at the table next to her, where a variety of items were spread out. 'One-stop shopping.'

'No, thank you,' Amina said. 'I need to sell a painting. Do you know who buys paintings in the market? Works by artists?'

The woman scratched her chin, thinking. She pointed. 'There are men who deal in art,' she said. 'Keep going down this street and ask the men just after that long table of bananas past the alley.'

Amina continued down the street in the direction the woman had pointed, pausing to look at a pile of golden rice spread on a plastic tarp on the street. She made a silent promise that she would return after she had sold Aabbe's painting and had a few shillings in her pocket. Rice might make all the difference in the world for Hooyo and the baby.

Streets crisscrossed the main thoroughfare, a labyrinth of streets, each one crowded with vendors. It would be easy to get lost. As she passed an alley, someone screamed and a glass bottle fell from one of the windows, shattering on the street below.

An African Union soldier stood on the street corner, holding his gun, a finger on the trigger. He watched Amina out of the corner of his eye as she hurried past. It made her think of Roble. Was he also holding a gun somewhere, finger on the trigger, manning roadblocks for al-Shabaab?

She shook the thought away as she passed the long table piled high with bananas, towards a group of men standing behind tables.

'I'm looking for somebody who buys paintings,' she said. 'Somebody told me you might be able to help me.'

One of the men stepped forward. He was tall and slender. Several tasbih dangled around his neck. The long strings of prayer beads made soft jangling noises whenever he moved. 'Yes, yes,' he said. 'My name is Dalmar. I can do business with you. What kind of painting do you have to sell?'

Amina swallowed, her mouth dry. She was nervous and stammered. 'I—I have a S-Samatar Khalid.' She unwrapped the painting and held it up so the men could see.

Dalmar leaned forward, inspecting the upper right-hand corner for her father's signature. That was where he always put it. 'Yes, I see this is an original.' He spoke in the voice of one making an official pronouncement.

'Who are you?' A man sitting at a table piled high with used clothing spoke then. 'You are not Samatar Khalid's usual dealer.' He was very fat and sweat glistened on his upper lip and even his eyelids. His eyes were half closed, as if he had been sleeping.

Amina hadn't thought about her status in the market, or the fact that buyers were used to dealing with only one person – Keinan's father. She raised her head, suddenly proud. They might question who she was but they all knew her father's work. 'He's my father,' she said.

'Ah, yes.' He examined her. It felt like a test. 'I see the resemblance now,' he said at last. 'In face. In spirit. You are definitely your father's child. Do you paint?'

She wondered if she should deny it because of al-Shabaab, but she saw no guile in his face. 'Sometimes,' she said. But she wasn't about to tell this man about her street art.

'Good,' he said.

She waited but the men were silent. 'So would you like to buy the painting?' she asked.

Dalmar glanced at the fat man as if waiting for him to respond but the fat man said nothing. 'Just step over to my shop then and we will have the painting appraised,' Dalmar said.

The fat man spoke. 'Samatar Khalids are worth money. I will buy it.' He named a price. Amina recognised that it was a lot of money – it would last them some time.

'No,' Dalmar said. 'He tells you one thing but you think he has that kind of money underneath his rotting table and his fraying cloth? I will give you double what he has offered.'

The fat man looked towards the ocean as if he had grown bored with the conversation. 'Take the money now,' he said, indifferent. 'If you go with him, my offer disappears.'

Amina clutched the painting, unsure what she should do.

Dalmar waved his hands. 'Look, look,' he said. 'We can all be happy here. You give me the painting. I will go to my shop – see, there? It is just three doors down. You see? You stay here. I will ask my boss what it is worth and then I will come back with more money than this man has offered. If I am wrong, you can give this man the painting and collect what he has offered.'

Amina looked from Dalmar to the fat man. The fat man clucked his tongue disapprovingly and stared off at the sky while Dalmar watched her expectantly. She handed the painting to Dalmar.

'One minute,' Dalmar promised. He ran down the street towards the shop he had indicated.

She didn't even realise she was holding her breath until she saw him turn into the shop he'd mentioned. She let it out. He'd been telling the truth – he would go into that shop. He wouldn't just disappear with the painting.

Still, she stood on her tiptoes, as though that would help her see him more quickly when he reappeared.

Amina waited for several minutes before she started growing nervous. She looked at the fat man.

He laughed. 'You should have taken me up on my offer, no?' he said. 'Now you have lost your father's painting *and* the money you would have got for it. Too bad. It was a good painting.'

Amina walked to the shop where the man had disappeared. Her whole body was tense. The shop was empty except for a boy Amina's age standing behind the counter, mobile phones displayed beneath the glass.

'May I help you?' he asked. 'You are looking for mobile phones?' He gestured at the display glass.

'Where is the man that came in here?' Amina asked. 'He was carrying a painting.'

The boy looked at her blankly.

'He was skinny,' she said. *Skinny, like a hyena*, she thought. *A hungry look on his face.* 'His name is Dalmar.'

'No,' the boy said.

Ayeeyo stared at him. 'No? No what?'

'No, I haven't seen him.'

'But I saw him come in here,' Amina said. She was a little louder, a little more insistent, than a girl should be. 'He walked right inside this door. Into this shop. He had the painting tucked under his arm. I watched him.'

'I'm sorry, but I haven't seen him.' He shrugged, unconcerned. 'There is no man named Dalmar here. There is no painting.'

She tried to look past him, into the dim room beyond, but he moved to block her view.

'How can I help you?' he asked. He didn't sound as friendly as before. 'Are you sure you don't need a mobile phone?'

Amina walked outside and looked at the streets

zigzagging away from the shop, the people meandering from shop to stall, looking at items for sale.

She had lost Aabbe's painting and they had lost the money an honest dealer might have paid for it.

Clouds skidded briskly across the bright blue sky. Amina shuffled around and around, circling faster and faster until she felt dizzy. She held out her arms towards the brilliance of the sun, the glare making the edges of the world go black, her heart aching with the raw grief of loss.

Staggering backwards, she almost fainted, but caught herself against a wall. Her body sagged into the dirt and dust. Though people stared at her curiously as they passed, no-one stopped.

It was true that it was only Aabbe's painting that had been hijacked, not Aabbe himself. He had been taken long ago now. Yet until this moment, Amina had been able to shove his painful absence to the back of her mind. She didn't know where the certainty had come from, but she had been confident that he would come home some day – just walk through the door, greeting Hooyo with his warm smile, chucking Amina under the chin as though she were a small girl, grinning at Roble.

Now the painting's unexpected loss had stolen her fragile hope. She suddenly felt sure that she would never see her father again.

Chapter 9

Ayeeyo told Amina it wasn't her fault. 'I should have been there to help,' she said. 'Of course, you are too trusting. You have never known anything but kindness.'

It didn't make Amina feel better, especially since Hooyo was not as understanding. When they returned and told her what had happened, she turned her face to the wall.

Ayeeyo placed a hand on Hooyo's shoulder and nodded at Amina that she should go.

Amina walked to the kitchen and sat on the floor near the clay pot, the ashes cold underneath. She listened to the sounds from her parents' bedroom – Ayeeyo murmuring and Hooyo babbling, a high, panicky tone to her voice. She poked aimlessly at the ashes with a cooking spoon. It occurred to her that ashes could be used to make paint but even that didn't make her feel better. The itch in her fingertips was gone, replaced by shaky hunger and a lost feeling, something deep inside quietly reminding her that it was all her fault.

Eventually the sounds in the other room subsided and Ayeeyo emerged. 'She's asleep,' she announced, as though that made everything better.

Amina nodded. She didn't trust herself to speak.

'I don't know what we're going to do,' Ayeeyo said honestly but without blame.

Amina thought about what they had gone through that day, all in an attempt to get money to buy food and medicine for Hooyo. She knew she couldn't return to the market. She couldn't bear that feeling of losing her father all over again. She wanted to hoard his paintings. You couldn't eat paintings, but as long as she had them, it felt as though Aabbe was still close. The paintings kept him alive.

She must find another path to help her family. But how? Everything felt hopeless and pointless. She directed a desperate prayer towards the sky. *Help us. Please help us.*

◆➤■◆

In the days that followed, Amina found that she rarely felt the hunger pains. The reality of having no food to eat and no way to help Aabbe, Roble or Hooyo pressed in from all sides. She scrounged the neighbourhood for free food and brought back a few small avocados, which she stole from a neighbour's tree. Though they were bland and unripe, the three women ate every bite. She found overripe bananas, the skin black and weeping, in a pile of rubbish. They ate those too.

Sometimes, she climbed the crumbling steps to the second floor and looked out at the city and the sparkling grey-blue of the ocean just beyond. She watched all the activity, the streets busier than she ever remembered seeing them. People came and went from Keinan's house, but she saw no sign of Keinan. Boys played a ferocious soccer game a few blocks away. A group of soldiers dressed in army fatigues and camouflaged helmets ran quickly down a dirt alley and disappeared into a hole in the ground. One afternoon, she saw what looked like three bodies lying in the middle of the street a few blocks over. By evening, the bodies had been removed.

Aabbe was out there somewhere.

And Roble was out there somewhere.

Who knew what Roble was being forced to do, just to survive? Two other boys she had known had disappeared from the neighbourhood, forced to be soldiers with al-Shabaab factions. One had made it back. Though he had lost an arm in battle and had been left behind, no longer useful as a soldier, he was still fiercely loyal to al-Shabaab. His mother lived in terror that he would report the family for some minor infraction and they would be subject to al-Shabaab's version of justice – swift, brutal and usually deadly. Amina couldn't imagine Roble changing that much. She couldn't imagine him succumbing to their brainwashing. And yet before he and Aabbe were taken, she couldn't have imagined life without them. And here she was.

Hooyo stayed in bed. She didn't even get up for prayers. Amina and Ayeeyo prayed alone and drank weak tea to still the hunger pains. After prayers, Amina retreated to Aabbe's studio for much of the day, instead of going to school or staying inside with her mother and grandmother. She blamed herself for everything, but it was easier to forget this when she was alone.

She sat in Aabbe's high stool, wondering what he was facing – wherever he was. She already knew the stories about what al-Shabaab did to the people they called infidels – scientists, clerics, artists like Aabbe. She had herself seen a corpse left in the street, headless, missing its arms and legs – al-Shabaab's handiwork.

She shivered and hoped Aabbe was all right. If anybody would escape, it had to be Aabbe. He was resourceful. And they needed him at home. Surely Allah would protect him.

She stared at his most recent painting, the ocean scene far from shore, the grey-green waves curling up and licking the stone grey sky. How did he do it? How did he make the waves sing and live? Her own drawings felt clunky and amateurish in comparison.

The small studio, its thick walls constructed with mud and sticks, was dark except for the small amount of natural light that fell through the open door and the tiny window. Hadn't Aabbe felt claustrophobic, sitting in this dusky light, day after day, painting? Why hadn't he gone outside? In here, he had been cut off from the world, painting only from memory or photographs.

Amina preferred to do her work in places where sunlight flooded through holes in the roof or where whole walls had been knocked over. If she was going to paint or draw at home, she would do it upstairs where the sky was the ceiling. But, of course, she would never use her own house as a canvas – no need to let Ayeeyo and Hooyo know what she was up to.

In any case, even if she felt the urge – which she didn't, not at the moment – she knew where she belonged. She had to stay here, making sure Hooyo and Ayeeyo were safe. Certainly she shouldn't be doing something dangerous, something many people considered haram, forbidden. Why had she ever thought she was called to create art? Nothing was more important than taking care of her family.

She had to give up her art.

◆▰◆

One afternoon a couple of weeks after they returned from the market, Amina stood up and fainted. Darkness closed around her, the world in front of her receding to a tiny pinprick and then disappearing from sight altogether. She came to on the floor of the studio. Her head throbbed and she could feel a swollen lump on her forehead where she had crashed against the hard-packed dirt.

It was the first time she had fainted from hunger.

She stood up and sat back down immediately when the dizziness returned. She waited until it passed and then stood up again, exiting the studio and heading towards the house.

As she entered, she heard Hooyo wheezing, short, high, fearful intakes of breath, over and over. She raced to her parents' bedroom. Ayeeyo was already kneeling beside the bed. Hooyo clutched her stomach.

Amina was shocked at how emaciated she looked. The hollow cheeks. Dark shadows under her eyes. A haunted look.

'What's wrong, Hooyo?' Amina asked.

Hooyo groaned.

'She needs to see a doctor,' Ayeeyo said.

'It's nothing,' Hooyo gasped. She closed her eyes. 'I don't need the doctor.'

Amina waited. Hooyo didn't open her eyes.

'She needs more to eat than what you've been able to find,' Ayeeyo said.

Amina went outside. She stood at the gate, watching the world go by. Ants marched past, carrying crumbs. At least they had something to eat.

Turning around and surveying the yard, she noticed the tender green shoots poking through the dirt. Weeds. Nothing but weeds. Were weeds edible?

A beetle crawled through a patch of weeds. Were beetles edible? Even more important, were they halal? Could she, as a devout Muslim, eat them in good conscience?

The thought of eating beetles made her feel nauseous.

But weeds – those were definitely halal. And they couldn't be that different from spinach or kale or lettuce, could they? Maybe the weeds would save them. Amina grabbed a bucket and began filling it.

She left the beetles alone. There would be time for harvesting bugs later, if and when they were truly starving. She would remember. Surely Allah would forgive them for eating non-halal foods, if it was a question of starving to death.

She took the bucket inside and held it out to her grandmother, an offering. 'Look, Ayeeyo,' she said. 'Do you think Hooyo will eat it?'

'If she won't, *we* will,' Ayeeyo said.

Ayeeyo's hands trembled as she placed the green stalks and spines inside a clay pot, with a little bit of water and the last of the salt. She lit a rounded pile of charcoal on the floor and waited until the charcoal was glowing red. Then she placed the clay pot on top of the coals, and they watched as the steam rose along with the odour of the boiled weeds.

If she weren't so hungry, the dank, swampy smell would have made Amina gag.

After sunset and Maghrib prayers, she took a plate of the greens in to Hooyo. They looked thoroughly unappetising – slick as sweat and slimy. They threatened to slide off the plate.

Hooyo was lying on her side, clutching her belly. Seeing the plate of greens, she moved into a sitting position. She balanced the plate on her lap and took a large bite, gagging slightly as the greens went into her mouth. But she swallowed and then sat there for a moment, as though gaining balance. Spittle gathered in the corners of her mouth.

She ate the whole plate quickly, gobbling, as though afraid the greens would disappear if she didn't eat them immediately. Or perhaps she was afraid she would lose her courage.

Ayeeyo had gone into the yard and cleared it of remaining weeds. Now she sat beside Amina in the kitchen. While the weeds cooked, they drank weak tea, reusing teabags and sticks of cinnamon and a few remaining grains of sugar. It was little more than water and left Amina's tastebuds unsatisfied, but somehow, the hot liquid soothed an ache in her stomach that had nothing to do with hunger.

As long as she was thinking about food, she wasn't thinking about Aabbe or Roble. Or Keinan.

Ayeeyo had just dished up bowls of the slippery boiled weeds when they heard Hooyo retching. Amina jumped up and ran to Hooyo, who was crouched by the side of the bed, sliding an arm around her and holding her head as she threw up the entire plate of weeds.

She wiped Hooyo's forehead with the edge of her scarf. In the kitchen, dishes clattered as Ayeeyo threw out the only meal they'd cooked in days.

◆▬◆

Amina joined Ayeeyo in the kitchen. They stared at the cooking pot in silence.

'What should we do?' Amina asked finally.

'Go,' Ayeeyo said. 'Go and ask the neighbours for something to eat. Tell them we cannot pay them now but we will pay later. Nothing is going to change if we just sit here inside the house and do nothing. The only thing that will happen is that we'll starve to death.'

Amina tied a scarf around her hair. She slipped outside the gate. It wasn't hunger she felt now. It was shame. How could she possibly tell the neighbours they were starving? How could she beg for food?

Keinan was in the street, dribbling a soccer ball between his feet. He glanced up when Amina walked out and opened his mouth, as if he was going to shout a greeting.

Amina turned away. She couldn't talk to Keinan now. She couldn't pretend that her family was well, yet she was ashamed to let him know that they were hungry.

'Hey!' he called after her. 'Amina!'

She hurried to get away.

'Amina!'

He jogged alongside her. She picked up her pace and wouldn't look at him. 'Hey! Amina!'

'What?' She met his eyes. A breath escaped her lips, harsh, shuddery even, as he drew his own breath in.

'What's wrong?' he asked.

'Nothing,' she said, though they both knew that was a lie. She felt a stab of anger that he would even ask such a question. Her father and brother were gone and he knew it. If he couldn't realise how that might make her family suffer, then he wasn't the person she thought he was.

'What are you doing?' he asked.

'I'm going to buy some food,' she lied.

'I'll come with you,' he said.

'I don't need your help,' she said. She bit her lip and kept walking fast. 'And we still shouldn't be walking together. My mother would kill me. But thank you,' she added, hoping it softened her words.

He stopped and soon she was ahead of him. She glanced back. He was standing in the middle of the street, soccer ball in the crook of his arm. She didn't understand the look on his face.

Tears bit the corners of her eyelids.

◆▰◆

Amina knocked on four neighbours' gates, shouting hello.

Two neighbours failed to answer her call.

One neighbour told her that it was hard for everybody. She wished she had food to give but she and her family had none themselves. 'We are planning to try the food relief camps,' she told Amina. 'I would suggest that you come with me but we don't know yet if it is safe. If al-Shabaab is around, those men will take a young, pretty girl like you and force you to become the wife of one of their commanders.'

As much as Amina's stomach hurt from hunger, fear still shot through her at those words. She would rather go hungry than be forced to become a 'wife' of an al-Shabaab soldier.

'But al-Shabaab left Mogadishu,' Amina protested.

The neighbour shook her head. 'You never can tell what might happen in this city. It's better to be safe and go hungry.'

'You can't do that forever,' Amina said.

'No, you can't,' the neighbour agreed.

Leaving that neighbour's house, she banged on the gate of yet another house. That neighbour gave her a small cup of cooked rice and apologised that it was all she had to give. 'Please don't tell anyone I gave you food,' she said. 'Or I'll wake up in the morning with the whole neighbourhood camped out here.'

Amina started home, wondering what she would tell Ayeeyo. At least the rice would help Hooyo. And the baby.

The baby no longer seemed real. It certainly wasn't as real as the constant, dull ache in Amina's stomach. The weakness in her muscles. The feeling that she would just like to lie down and never get up. The pervasive worry and dread that crept through her bones like arthritis.

What if Hooyo lost the baby, all because she hadn't had enough to eat? There was no return from something like that.

She told no-one but that day, before she went home, she decided to go to the market. When a woman selling canjeero turned around for just a second, Amina snatched a stack of the flatbread and ran home.

She had become a thief. What would Ayeeyo say if she knew? What would Hooyo say?

She could never tell them. This would be her secret, always. She could hardly believe it herself.

She let herself into the yard and locked the gate behind her, gripping the cup of rice and stack of canjeero.

◆▶■◀◆

After eating, Hooyo had revived for a few minutes. She sat up and asked Amina to bring her a book. Now she was reading and Amina was watching. Hovering. She knew that she was bothering Hooyo, but she couldn't help it.

'Let's name the baby,' Amina said. She sat on the edge of the mat that Hooyo had shared with Aabbe, picking at the blanket, looking at the floor and waiting to hear her response.

Hooyo placed the book down on the blankets. 'It's too early. We don't even know if it's a boy or girl.'

'It's a girl,' Amina said impulsively. 'I know it.' She felt bad as soon as she said it. She *didn't* know it. She was just trying, as hard as she could, to cling to the reality of the baby.

As long as the baby survives, she suddenly thought, *we'll all survive.*

She looked at Hooyo's deflated stomach, Hooyo who had lost weight during her pregnancy instead of gaining it the way she should have. Hooyo looked old, too old to be having a baby. Amina was the one who should be having a baby. She was old enough to be married, *she* could be the one giving birth. She was young. Even if she was suffering from malnutrition, *her* baby would survive a time of hunger, war, anything. But Hooyo's?

'Are you too old to have a baby?' Amina asked. *Is the baby going to be all right?* That's what she wanted to ask. *Are you going to be all right, Hooyo? Are you going to survive?*

Hooyo laughed. 'What are you talking about, Amina? I'm only thirty-six.'

'That's old,' Amina said.

Hooyo rubbed her temples, thumb on one side, index finger on the other. 'Amina, in some parts of the world, I'm still considered a young woman.'

121

'What are *you* talking about, Hooyo?' Amina teased. '*I'm* the young woman!'

Hooyo reached over and touched Amina's hand. She laughed. 'Yes, you are, daughter. Yes, you are.'

Amina stared at Hooyo. 'So, aren't you too old to have a baby?'

'I'm not too old, it'll be all right.' Hooyo sighed. 'I just need more food. Better food. Real nourishment. This—' She looked around at the empty room, down at the tiny bulge in her belly. 'This situation is not ideal.' Then she laughed, shortly, at the understatement in her words.

'That's why I want to give the baby a name,' Amina said. She didn't know how to ask Hooyo for the thing she needed more than anything. She didn't have a word for it herself.

Hooyo shivered. 'No,' she said. 'Let's wait.'

'It'll be fun,' Amina persisted, knowing she was pushing it. 'We can think about both boy and girl names. I like Jamilah.' Amina had a classmate whose name was Jamilah. Jamilah was pretty and kind and popular. Amina had always wanted to be friends with her.

'No!' Hooyo's voice was sharp. 'I said, *let's wait.*'

Amina's hopes deflated. She left the bedroom and stood in the dark kitchen, her fingers twitching aimlessly. She wanted to do something. She wanted—

Ayeeyo came into the kitchen. 'Don't let her upset you,' she said. 'She's just afraid.'

Amina nodded. She was afraid too. Why did Hooyo get to wallow all day in her misery while Amina had to be the strong one?

Chapter 10

As she stepped outside the gate to search for food – or to steal it – Amina heard a familiar, gravelly voice behind her. 'Asalaam Alaykum, peace be upon you, Amina.'

She froze. Legs shaking, she turned to face him. Abdullahi Hassan, Keinan's father, the man responsible for Aabbe's arrest and disappearance. But he was also the man who helped protect her and Ayeeyo from the men who stalked them on the way to the market. She was still afraid, even though he probably didn't wish to harm her.

Though he and Keinan resembled each other, there was something different about Abdullahi Hassan's face. Amina thought human faces were like houses. Some had lots of windows, letting in the light. Others were like a solid brick wall, hiding everything. Keinan was boastful and proud, but his eyes were like skylights, flooding a house with the sun. His father had little slits for eyes that took in light but reflected nothing.

'Wa 'Alaykum Asalaam, and peace be upon you as well,' she greeted him.

'How is your family?' he asked. His eyes flicked over her. 'How are your mother and grandmother?'

'They are fine, adeer,' Amina said politely. 'Thank you for asking.'

'I was sorry to hear about your father.'

Amina choked. She found she could not speak so she nodded in response, then looked at the dirt. She could not look this man in the eye, with his pretend warmth and compassion. He was Muslim, Somali and a neighbour – but he was no friend and no brother.

This was one of the hard lessons that Amina had learned in the last few months – how even people who shared your faith, your language and your culture could still betray you.

'And your brother, too. Your family has met with many misfortunes this year. I am sorry for your troubles. Should you need anything, you must come and we will help you.'

'Thank you.' Amina stared at his expensive shoes. She didn't know a lot about fashion but she could tell they were expensive. Somali businessmen could get anything, anywhere, anytime, if they had the money.

'My people tell me one of your father's paintings was filtered through Bakaara recently.'

'Maybe,' she said.

'If you need to sell one of your father's paintings, I can help,' he said.

'We're fine.' She brimmed with anger.

'I also hear that you may be an artist yourself?'

Amina stared resentfully at him. Where had he heard that? Had Keinan told him? 'I don't know what you're talking about,' she said. 'I'm not an artist.' It hurt to say that, but it was true. She'd given it up.

'I could perhaps help you sell your pieces,' he said.

Amina didn't respond. She waited for him to leave so she could go.

He sighed loudly, as though Amina had disappointed him. As though she had let him down. But Amina didn't care. She didn't trust him, not for one second.

◆➤■◆

Amina lurked near the neighbourhood market daily. Though she didn't beg for food and money from strangers, she was beginning to feel like one of the street kids, snatching up food scraps from the dirt.

Sometimes she was lucky enough to find cast-off bread or vegetables or even a piece of fish, slimy and decomposing. They sorted through everything at home, throwing away anything that was too rotten to eat, ignoring the slightly mouldy taste of everything else.

Sometimes, to her shame, and only as a last resort, she took something – if a back was turned. Amina knew that was dangerous. If somebody caught her, she'd be branded a thief and might lose a hand or a foot or both. She might never be able to paint again, but hunger and need overruled her concern.

One day, she ran into Basra and her mother near the market.

'Amina!' Basra cried. 'How are you?'

Amina was surprised at the way Basra's eyes lit up when they greeted each other. Despite the kindness in sharing her food, she had never supposed that Basra really liked her.

'I'm fine,' she replied. 'How are you?'

She hid her basket behind her back, ashamed of the rotting food inside. Their basket was stuffed with bananas, tomatoes, carrots and onions. Amina's mouth watered.

'Where have you been?' Basra shifted, her hand holding steady the jar of camel's milk that she carried on her head. 'You've missed a lot of school. Are you sick?'

'No, I've been needed at home,' she said, echoing what she had told Basra a few weeks earlier about Roble. With everything that had happened to her family, school had seemed impossibly distant, part of a normal life that no longer existed for her.

Basra's mother looked concerned. 'Is your mother well?'

'Everything's fine,' Amina said. She had to protect her family's reputation. It was impossible to know who you could trust. 'But our family will grow larger soon and Hooyo's on bed rest. She's needed more help.'

Basra clapped her hands together. 'You must be so excited.'

'Your family is blessed,' Basra's mother agreed.

'But you have to come back to school,' Basra said.

Amina nodded. 'I'll try.'

Basra's mother turned away but Basra paused, leaning back and whispering, 'We're writing poetry next week. The teacher said we will have a competition in class – girls against boys. You're the best. We need you.'

Amina smiled, happy that she'd been missed. 'I'll be there.'

'Promise,' Basra said.

'Promise,' Amina agreed. She would do her best to keep that promise.

Basra leaned forward, as though she wanted to share a secret. Amina leaned forward, too, until their head-scarfs touched.

'Don't give up,' Basra whispered.

Amina straightened up. 'Thank you,' she said.

They waved goodbye and Amina hurried towards her house, something other than endless despair spreading warmly throughout her body. *Don't give up*, Basra had said.

The words echoed in her head. *Don't give up.*

◆▬◆

Amina let herself into the yard and started towards the house. Something thudded against the gate. She fell to her knees, wondering if they were under attack. Crouching low, she inched over to the wall and peeked out through the cracks.

Somebody had left a small cloth-covered basket in front of the gate.

Gently, she eased the gate open. What if it was a bomb?

She looked left and right, and saw what she thought might be the figures of Basra and her mother disappearing around a corner. Her heart beat fast.

She snatched the basket and whisked it inside, leaning against the wall as she examined its contents. It contained a jar, a big bunch of bananas and several avocados. It was all Amina could do to keep herself from seizing the entire bunch of bananas and gobbling them down. She peeked at the white liquid inside the jar, dipped a finger in, and tasted it. Camel's milk! In the very same jar Basra had carried on her head just minutes ago.

She ran inside, shouting that a friend from school had left food in front of the house.

Ayeeyo fixed Hooyo a bowl of sliced bananas and camel's milk, lightly heated on the bed of coals. Amina perched nearby, ready to devour the food. 'Don't overeat or your stomach will reject it,' Ayeeyo cautioned Amina. 'Go slow.'

Amina split a banana in two, ate half, and set aside the other half for Ayeeyo. She drank half a cup of milk with sugar in it. Nobody drank camel's milk that way – but Amina had never cared for the sour taste so her mother had sweetened it ever since she was little.

She sat quietly to see how her stomach would react.

The chance encounter with Basra and her mother, Basra's desire for Amina to come back to school and the unexpected gift of food had changed something. Amina wasn't sure what it was until she felt the itch in her fingertips. That unquenchable urge, which she thought she had lost forever. It was swelling to the point of bursting.

Don't give up.

She wouldn't. In fact, what could she do right now, today? *Something for Aabbe*, she thought. Then, *No, something for Roble.*

◆➤■◆

When Ayeeyo and Hooyo were both having an afternoon nap, Amina tied a scarf around her head, slipped a charcoal pencil in her pocket, and sneaked out of the house. She closed the gate gently behind her and looked left and right. The street was empty. She decided to go left.

Three or four abandoned or burnt-out buildings lay in that direction, including an old shopfront. Amina remembered going there when she was younger. The shopkeeper's wife made halwa and Aabbe would often buy some for Amina. They would walk home together, slowly, while she savoured the jellied sugar melting in her mouth, traces of nutmeg and cardamom lingering on the tip of her tongue.

Her heart pounded as slipped inside the shop's crumbling walls. Inside, she composed a short letter to Roble using a stick of charcoal.

Dear R.,
Hooyo stays quiet and prays all day long. We don't talk about you but we think about you all the time. We wonder where the soldiers took you and if you are still alive. I told her the baby will be a girl but I think she

wants another boy because she's afraid you won't come back. You didn't choose to leave us. Maybe you can't return. Maybe the soldiers keep you captive or maybe they've taught you to hate us because we don't support what they stand for. But we love you no matter what. Aabbe is also still missing. We have no food. We have no money. Yet we hope and pray that at least you are well fed and warm at night and that you don't forget us, just as we will never forget you. Come home. We're waiting.

Your sister,

A.

Amina filled in the gaps around the letter with short curling designs – vines and flowers. And, of course, her signature Somali star.

Could the letter help save Roble? Or, if not Roble, some other boy? She had to believe that if the right person saw it, they could do something. As much as she loved Ayeeyo, she could no longer believe a person's entire life was destined by Allah. No. She believed that Allah knew everything and had blessed humanity by giving them choices to make. She believed anybody could act and change the course of the world, whether in small ways or in large ways, and that a person was accountable to Allah for the choices they made, good or evil, in the afterlife. That was what Aabbe had believed. If it wasn't true, his work wouldn't have mattered and it would have all been for nothing.

She, too, was an artist. She couldn't help it. This was

her way of being in the world, her way of helping her city, her people and her family. So she would hope against hope that it would make a difference.

◆➤■◆

Every few days, Amina would hear the thump of a rock thrown against the gate. When she went to open it, she would find a basket of grain or pasta and bananas. Of course, it wasn't enough, and Amina still had to search near the market for leftover or discarded scraps of food. Some of the women had taken pity on her and would save food for her – a dried fish or a couple of potatoes.

Amina had returned to school and Basra was sharing her food. Amina had noticed that Basra was packing larger amounts of food than she used to. She didn't comment – she just let Basra know she was thankful.

Amina was grateful to the people who were watching out for them. But it was never enough. Amina, who had always been thin, now felt fragile, skeletal.

On the days she went to school, Amina would make quick side-trips while walking home. Everything and anything was a canvas. A partially crumbling alley wall. A shopkeeper's signpost. The interior or exterior of an abandoned building. A stray rock.

On the weekends, she waited until Ayeeyo had lain down for a nap. Then she sneaked out, guilty and furtive but grateful for the freedom.

Ayeeyo never questioned where she went or why. Either she didn't know or she had realised the futility of scolding her granddaughter.

Amina started collecting bits and pieces on her excursions and bringing them back to the house – a piece of coloured glass, a bullet casing, an empty glasses frame, a trigger that had broken off from a gun, pieces of fabric. She left the detritus in her father's studio. Each time she returned with something new, she stared at the odds and ends, wondering what artwork she could make with them.

She returned to the abandoned building where she had first shown Keinan her work and found that the mud sculpture and mosaic were gone. She had thought she might take the mosaic to Bakaara and try to sell it.

Her drawing of the boys playing soccer was still intact, which startled her. Even more surprising, graffiti was scrawled across the wall. She wondered why, until she started reading the messages people had left.

> Somali soccer forever!
> You can break the body but not the spirit.
>
> Hey A! Come to our neighbourhood (Hodan)
> and draw us playing soccer.
> We have the best soccer players in all Mogadishu.
>
> We will have a normal life again, insha' Allah.
> Our boys will play soccer again.
> Hope, peace, love.

Amina smiled, a soft glow spreading through her entire body. She had done something worth paying attention to. Something of the spirit of freedom and peace had seeped through her work.

But now she looked at it with a critical eye. The perspective was off, and the boys' torsos were too long. She was tempted for just a minute to do something to fix it, but then she shook off the feeling.

Don't look back, she thought, reminding herself of the words Aabbe had told her so long ago – just a few short months, really, but it felt like years. *Don't get stuck in the here and now. Just look ahead.*

◆━━◆

One picture she drew whenever and wherever she could – a picture of her father, with the message she had initially written underneath it:

Samatar Khalid, taken from his home in Mogadishu.
One of many.

Poems flowed from her hand. She etched them on walls everywhere.

For the city of Mogadishu,
the city of sand and ocean and guns,
salt in the air, trees shaking in the wind, dirt alleys
and a maze of streets going this way and that.
Let Allah's peace and love settle on us
coating everything like dust in the rubble.

She signed everything with her signature A. and the Somali star. Would anybody ever see her poems? Maybe. But it didn't matter. She did this because Allah had given her the vision to do it, because of the itch in her fingertips, because she had things in her heart that needed to be expressed – not because somebody might see them. Allah saw them and perhaps that was all that mattered – to convey the message of love and peace through her artwork.

They were her prayers for the city of her birth.

Still, though she kept working, whenever and however she could, she had begun to feel uneasy. She'd gone back to a few of her original sites and found work missing – the smaller pieces she did, like the cloth or glass mosaics.

Maybe she should stop. If she didn't, she might end up with a similar fate as her father.

One day, while squatting inside an abandoned building and sketching a poem on its interior walls, she caught a glimpse of something moving in the corner of her eyes. She stood swiftly and scanned the street just in time to spot Keinan slipping behind a freestanding wall to hide.

The glow she felt from working was quickly eaten up by fear. She'd decided to trust Keinan the day she'd gone to the market with Ayeeyo, but maybe she had been too hasty. Why was he following her?

She never should have told him about her work. Was he spying on her for his father? Would al-Shabaab come and take her away too?

She ran home, determined to be more careful the next time she worked.

Because there would always be a next time, now.

Chapter 11

'**We have to take one** of your father's paintings and try again,' Ayeeyo said one day. 'Allah has blessed us with food that someone has generously given but now we must do what we can to take care of ourselves.'

Her words hit Amina like a grenade, a hot, searing light exploding inside her.

'Now we know how to find the Bakaara Market and now we know what to expect,' Ayeeyo said. 'We must forgive the one who did us wrong but that doesn't mean we have to trust people.'

Amina nodded, quietly agreeing. She had lost nearly everything that day but the worst thing of all was that she'd nearly lost herself. Now that she was working again – painting or writing almost every day – she realised she was most herself when she was working on her art. And she'd nearly given it up for good.

'You're right, Ayeeyo,' Amina said. 'I will enter the market like a lion.'

She felt like a lion. A lion recovering from a battle

that had left her bruised and shaken, but not beaten.

She went to her father's studio. She looked through the stack of paintings he had finished, wishing with all her heart that she could keep them. But she had to let go. She just hoped that it didn't feel like she was letting go of Aabbe too.

It's not the same, it's not, she told herself. *I have to go. If I wasn't doing this, Aabbe would be doing it or Roble.* One way or the other, Aabbe's paintings would have ended up in other people's hands.

She selected her least favourite painting, the one of Bakaara Market. If she had to part with one, she'd part with the one she liked the least. She'd keep doing that until, well, until she had no more paintings left to sell.

By then, perhaps her own work would be good enough that she could start selling it. She wasn't entirely sure how she felt about that – she wanted her work to be accessible to everybody. But the family needed to survive somehow. And she'd rather sell her work than continue to steal.

Tucking the painting under her jalbaab, she went inside to say goodbye to Ayeeyo and Hooyo.

'I should go with you,' Ayeeyo said.

'No,' Amina said. 'Remember last time, how you got sunstroke? And now you are even weaker, with even less food in your belly.' She didn't mention the arthritis that kept Ayeeyo awake at night and made her steps slow and painful. 'I will go alone and I will succeed this time.'

She spoke bravely but her stomach ached, though

not with hunger. The hunger pains no longer bothered her because they were constant. This ache was fear.

◆▶◀◆

Amina retraced the path they had taken when they followed Keinan and his father to Bakaara, then headed straight to the place where she had been swindled the last time. She pretended to be confident, but she hoped she wouldn't see Dalmar. She wanted to believe she would be brave and shout *thief* if she saw him, but she knew she would just slink away and go home instead, failing to sell the painting and facing Ayeeyo's disappointment.

She walked down the street, passing the red, blue and orange umbrellas, the African Union soldiers in fatigues, tables piled high with limes and carrots and capsicums.

She could practically taste the relief when she arrived and saw the fat man sitting at the table with a woman, probably his wife. No Dalmar in sight. Relief tasted strangely like blood until Amina realised she was so stressed that she had bitten her tongue.

'I have another Samatar Khalid,' Amina said. 'Are you interested?'

The fat man acknowledged her with his chin. 'I'll buy it,' he said. 'I can always sell Samatar Khalids. Let me see it.'

Amina pulled out Aabbe's painting of Bakaara Market, with its dual images of the massive mosque and the men trading gigantic guns.

The fat man coughed. 'Hide that, quick,' he said.

Amina immediately sheathed it beneath the fabric of her jalbaab. 'Don't you like it?' she asked.

'Oh, it's good,' he said. 'But it's dangerous, at least around here. There are still some secret al-Shabaab operatives who work here.' He shook his head.

'Buy it. It'll sell,' his wife said.

He named a price similar to the one he had suggested for the last painting that Amina had brought him. She agreed quickly. He lifted a hand and crooked his index finger. Within a few seconds, a young man wandered over to him. He leaned close and the fat man spoke quietly into his ear. Curious, the young man glanced at Amina, then left.

'Let me tell you what's become really popular the last few weeks,' the fat man said. 'We've sold a couple of pieces by someone we've started calling the "Artist". If you can get your hands on one of *his* pieces of art—'

'Who's the Artist?' Amina asked. She was curious, of course, but getting her hands on another artist's work was beyond her. It was all she could do to sell her father's paintings.

'Nobody knows,' he said.

'He doesn't have a name?'

'He's a street artist; some people might call what he does very good graffiti. He signs his work with the letter A. and the Somali star. Everybody's talking about him. I could sell one of his works in five minutes.'

Amina's face got very hot, so hot she was sure he could see the panic on it. 'How do you know it's a boy?' she managed to ask.

The man's wife shook her head, the look on her face half admiring and half disapproving. 'A girl wouldn't take such risks. He's in trouble, that one.'

'The Artist?'

'Yes. Al-Shabaab is very angry, I hear.'

'But the African Union ran al-Shabaab out of the city.'

'Don't be fooled,' the man said. 'They still control some neighbourhoods. And they're still here. They might be walking around the market in disguise, looking just like you and me. They're just waiting to wreak havoc. We haven't heard the last of them, you'll see.'

'Why don't they like the Artist's work?' Amina spoke quickly. She knew she shouldn't ask but she had to know. Then she could decide exactly how scared she should be.

'Oh, they say he is working against Allah's will for Somalia.' He shrugged. 'They think his work is un-Islamic.'

'They probably think all artwork is un-Islamic,' Amina said.

'Yes. They are extremists.'

'And you? What do you think?'

'Me? I don't care about art. I just want to make money.'

At least he was honest. 'So if he is a street artist, how do you sell his work?' she asked.

'The Artist does other work, not just graffiti on buildings.' He laughed. 'We've seen mosaics, paintings, work made with things you could just find in the street... cast-off materials like strips of cloth or coloured glass.'

139

Amina felt a jolt of anger. So that was where her smaller pieces had gone when they'd disappeared. Even though she had been considering selling her own work, she still wasn't sure she wanted her work to be bought and displayed in people's homes. She wanted it to be available for everybody in Somalia, at least to anybody who discovered it where she had left it. And if somebody else brought her artwork in and sold it, that meant they were making money – while she and *her* family went hungry.

'People sometimes bring his work in and sell it to us. Some have even brought in imitations, but you can tell the difference,' the woman said.

'The Artist isn't trained,' the man said. 'His work is good, not great. But it's distinct.'

His wife spoke up. 'It's sincere. It's real. People need that. Somalia needs it.'

'Why?' Amina asked.

'It's the spirit behind the work,' the woman explained. 'People gravitate towards it. It's so—innocent. And idealistic. All the works that I've seen have this hope in them, a belief that we can change.'

'Maybe you shouldn't be selling them,' she said. 'Maybe people should just leave the Artist's work where they find it. That way, more people will see it.'

The man snorted. 'Idealism and money don't make good company, girl.'

'Maybe it's not about money,' she said.

He waved his hand, dismissing her. 'What would you know about it?'

The young man had returned with a pouch. The fat man reached under his table and pulled out a large black plastic bag. 'Here, hide the Samatar Khalid in that.'

Amina fumbled to put the painting into the plastic bag and handed it to the man as he gave her the pouch containing money. Amina counted it, noting that it was all there, just as he promised.

'You see, I am honest, not like that man you dealt with last time.'

'Dalmar.'

'Yes, Dalmar. Bakaara Market is full of con artists.' He searched her face for something. 'Your father is quite an artist,' he said. 'And a brave man. Brave or stupid. What about you?'

'Are you asking if I'm brave or stupid?' Amina asked.

He sniggered, his belly jiggling. 'Clearly, you are both brave *and* stupid or you wouldn't be *here*. Last time, you told me you paint sometimes. Are you an artist? Are you following in your father's footsteps?'

Amina stifled her immediate response, a shouted, *Yes!*

What could she say that would be the truth but would not reveal her identity as the elusive 'Artist' he had just been praising? She was an artist, at least she wanted to believe she was and his comments about the reputation of the Artist confirmed it. He hadn't been overly complimentary about her style or skill, but he had recognised the spirit in her work, and that made her proud.

Still, her work was nothing like Aabbe's.

'No,' she said finally. 'I'm not following in my father's footsteps.'

'Ah,' he said. 'Too bad. Somalia needs another Samatar Khalid. Well, perhaps you have a brother who will follow in his father's footsteps.'

She hid the pouch under the jalbaab, taking out just enough money to buy some food. She found a few bananas, some rice, tomatoes, potatoes, an onion and some goat meat. The meat was expensive, but worth it. She imagined Hooyo eating it and growing strong and healthy, and the baby too.

She did some sums in her head. Should she walk home and risk getting robbed? Or should she shell out precious money for a taxi?

The sun was low on the horizon. The last thing she wanted was to walk home in the dark, when anything could happen.

She joined a group getting into the taxi, a white minibus, squeezing in tight between two large women, grateful for once that she was thin. One of the women carried a chicken on her lap. A few men climbed on top and sat on the roof rack.

The taxi driver honked his horn impatiently at another taxi, then jerked out into traffic, swerving through intersections and hurtling down side alleys, narrowly avoiding small cars and trucks racing towards them. Amina wondered how the men sitting on top were managing to hold on.

The taxi shuddered to a stop one block from Amina's house. She jostled her way to the front to get off.

Dusk was falling. The sky seared crimson as the sun set on the horizon. Clouds trailed out over the ocean's edge. The sunset reflected off houses and walls, basking the entire neighbourhood in a warm, pink glow.

She felt practically giddy, dancing up the stone steps and into the house, ready to shout that everything would be all right now. She had food, lots of it, and money, lots of it, too. The family would survive and grow. Hooyo could eat like a queen for the rest of her pregnancy.

She skidded to a stop in the front room. Something smelled terrible – a heavy, thick odour.

Hooyo's bedroom door was closed. She heard a low, keening moan coming from behind it.

She tiptoed towards the room and opened the door.

Ayeeyo was hovering between the bedside and a pan of pink water. Hooyo sat straight up in bed, partially clothed, her eyes wide and bright with fear, her bloody hands uselessly trying to staunch the flow seeping from below her abdomen.

Chapter 12

'Go away!' Hooyo sobbed when she saw Amina. 'Go away.' She was so weak, her attempts to push Amina away felt like gentle pats, a bird's wing fluttering against her.

As she backed away, Amina's eyes met Ayeeyo's. Amina nodded, to let her know the trip had been successful, and she saw Ayeeyo's shoulders droop in grateful relief.

Amina shut the door gently behind her, lingering, ear close to the door. She could only hear Ayeeyo's quiet murmur and Hooyo's whimpered 'No, no, no,' in response.

Night fell quickly, the darkness heavy and suffocating. She couldn't stay there, listening to Hooyo's cries. She had to get out.

She climbed the crumbling stairs to the second floor, standing close to the edge, where part of the wall still remained. She leaned against it, looking out at the deep black horizon, the ocean at night. Stars were all that revealed where the ocean ended and the sky began. She took off her headscarf and the warm, salty breeze blew through her hair. Somebody was playing music nearby and the heavy *doof-doof* combined with the sounds of cars revving and the loud voices of two men walking past.

Amina fingered the money pouch clutched in her hands, trying hard not to think about the bloodstained sheets or the way Hooyo's fists were pressing hard to try to keep the blood back or maybe to keep the baby from coming too soon. Amina wasn't sure which.

She rubbed her eyes with her knuckles and waited.

Aabbe. Roble. Where are you? Please come home. We need you.

'Amina!' Ayeeyo stood at the foot of the stairs. Her voice was strained and, though she was doing her best to sound calm, Amina could hear a note of panic.

She ran down the stairs. 'How is Hooyo?'

'The flow of blood has stopped for now but I think we must take her to hospital.'

Amina's heart sank but she wasn't surprised. 'The baby's coming?'

'We could deliver the baby, but the amount of blood…and the pain she's having…' Ayeeyo shook her head. 'She needs to see a doctor.'

They went into the bedroom.

Hooyo was slumped on the mat, head tilted sideways, chin resting on her chest. Her hand was placed on her belly. She jerked up at their approach and, when she saw Amina, she grabbed her hand.

145

'Daughter,' she said.

That simple word melted the knot of anxiety Amina usually felt around her mother. She squeezed Hooyo's hand. 'I'm here, Hooyo. Is the baby coming too early?'

'It's early but not too early,' Hooyo said. 'I have so much scarring from my circumcision...it makes giving birth difficult.' She took deep breaths in between each word. 'I need to see a doctor. But I can't go to the hospital, it's a terrible place – so many patients and not enough nurses or doctors. I'm as likely to die as I am to get help. I can't give birth there. I want you to go to my friend Rahmo's house and bring her here to help.'

'Rahmo?' Amina asked.

'You met her a couple of times,' Hooyo said. 'We worked together at the hospital. You visited her house with me once. Do you remember? You liked her cats.'

Amina remembered the visit but only vaguely.

'She doesn't live too far,' Hooyo said. 'But we haven't visited for a while. The situation with al-Shabaab...' Her voice trailed off.

'Why don't we call her?' Amina asked.

'She doesn't have a phone.' Hooyo shifted, grimacing. 'She retired a few years ago so she is probably at home. If she's not, return quickly. It's going to be a long night and I need you here.'

'But—' Amina's objection was cut off by Hooyo's sudden cry.

Hooyo slid down on the mat and closed her eyes. She put her index finger in her mouth and bit down hard, as though it helped with the pain.

Ayeeyo saw the doubt in Amina's eyes and pushed her in the direction of the front door. 'Go. Quickly now.'

Amina grabbed the mobile phone that they used for emergencies, tied a scarf around her head, and took some of the money from the pouch before handing it to Ayeeyo. Her body felt like it was jumping out of her skin.

Ayeeyo followed her out into the yard and to the gate. 'Be careful,' she said. 'Here. Take this.' She handed Amina a small knife, the one she used to peel and pare potatoes. 'Keep it hidden but in your hand, like this.' She demonstrated, her fist closed around the handle, her sleeve hiding the blade.

Amina took the knife and hid it. It didn't make her feel safe. After all, if somebody had a gun, she would be outmatched.

'Keep to the shadows and hide,' Ayeeyo continued.

Amina nodded quickly. She wanted to leave. The conversation was only making her even more nervous about the journey.

◆▬◆

Amina ran the length of the street before she heard somebody calling her name. She jumped, whirling around and gripping the knife beneath her sleeve.

It was Keinan.

His eyes revealed equal measures of gladness to see her and worry about something. 'I was coming to find you,' he said. 'My father found out who you are, what you do.'

'What do you mean?'

'He knows you're the person doing all the graffiti work in the neighbourhood.'

'How did he find out? Did you tell him?'

'No.' Keinan sounded defensive. 'I wouldn't do that. He's been watching your family for years, ever since he started selling your aabbe's paintings.'

What should I do? Amina wondered. The important thing right now was Hooyo. She had to get help, no matter what. 'I can't think about this tonight,' Amina said.

'You need to hide,' Keinan urged. 'Those men who arrested your father are on their way here, and they intend to arrest you too.'

Fear crawled snake-like down Amina's spine. 'I'm leaving now,' she said.

'Good,' he said. 'Where are you going? Is it somewhere you can stay? You shouldn't come back, not for a while.'

'But Hooyo—'

'They're not coming for your mother.' He glanced behind him, as though expecting to see them. 'She'll be fine. They'll leave her alone.'

'I'm going right now to get a nurse for Hooyo,' she said. 'It's bad. The baby—'

'I'll go with you,' he interrupted. 'And I'll bring the nurse back.'

'No!' she said. And then she startled, as though she had heard a gun firing.

A trio of men were running towards them, shouting, 'Amina? Is that you?'

'Go, get out of here!' Keinan said.

Amina didn't stop to think. She held the jalbaab above her ankles so she wouldn't trip and ran into the darkness of the alley, hoping nobody would be waiting for her there. The moon lit a path down the centre of the alley. It was deserted.

She crouched in the darkness, half-hidden behind a crumbling wall, and waited until the men ran past, down the alley and towards the main street. Then she crept slowly back towards the street she had just come from, back against the wall, keeping out of the moonlight.

She edged around the corner. Far down the street, a woman was walking with her husband, holding a baby. In the other direction, she saw two boys juggling a soccer ball between them.

She started running towards the boys, as fast as she could go, keeping close to the wall, where it was darker. The boys stopped what they were doing and stared at her. One of them shouted, 'Where are you going?' but she didn't stop. Somebody was running after her. Feet pounded against the dirt road, out of sync with her own footsteps, and gaining on her.

She stopped, spinning around, brandishing the knife.

'Hey, it's only me!' Keinan shouted, skidding to a stop and holding up his hands.

Amina glared at him. 'How do I know I can trust you?' Her voice shook.

He closed his eyes, the skylights shuttered, blocking out the sun. 'Because it's *me*,' he said, wounded, like she'd actually stabbed him with the knife.

'I have to go,' she said. She hid her knife and walked briskly away.

'I'm coming too.' He jogged after her.

'No,' she said. 'Leave me alone.'

'I want to help.'

She ignored him but he stuck closely beside her as she ran down the street and turned right onto a cross street. Though she was still risking being found alone with Keinan, who wasn't her brother or even her cousin, she knew she was safer with him on the dangerous streets of Mogadishu at night. And yet she couldn't shake the sense of betrayal. She knew it was wrong to blame the son for the sins of the father – but blood ties were strong. If he had to choose, wouldn't Keinan always side with his family? Would he really choose to sacrifice his clan, his family, to save her? She couldn't believe it, not for a second. She would keep him close now, but if she had a chance to escape from him, she would.

'Wait,' Keinan hissed.

'What?' Amina stopped, abruptly.

'It's my father,' he whispered, gesturing to indicate his father walking down the street, a few houses away.

They stepped between a tree and a wall and waited. Amina held her breath. She'd never noticed how loud her breathing was until she needed to keep perfectly quiet.

A plastic cup rattled down the street, blown by a sudden wind.

She blinked. The moonlight seemed suddenly harsh, too bright. She let her breath out sharply. Her shadow – deformed and unrecognisable, but still *her shadow* – was leaking out onto the street, visible to anybody walking by.

What if Abdullahi Hassan had seen it? She pulled further behind the tree and held her breath again.

She glanced at the boy by her side. What if he shouted to his father and revealed she was there? What if—

Her mobile phone rang, a single, shrill note. Amina fumbled to pull it out, then pushed at the buttons desperately, her fingers clumsy, useless. Keinan grabbed the phone from her and silenced it.

'It's okay.' Keinan handed the phone back. 'He's too far away to hear it.'

They waited until Keinan's father was out of sight. Then they sneaked quietly in the other direction, turned a corner, and started to run. Amina peeked at the phone. Ayeeyo had called, probably to find out what was taking her so long. She would return the call when they reached Rahmo's house safely and she knew help was on its way.

'Do you know where you're going?' Keinan asked.

Amina stopped and held up a hand, bent over and wheezing. She wasn't used to running. 'It's just a few blocks over,' she said. 'It's not far.'

'Let's keep going,' he said.

For a moment, Amina was glad for his presence. He had saved her twice now. Maybe she could trust him after all.

They trudged down the long street, glancing left and right, eyes roving restlessly, seeking any sudden move-ment from the other people who were out late, travelling from one place to another. A fire was burning down one alley, a group of street kids clustered around it. They passed a woman huddling in the shelter of an abandoned house, shielding two small children with her long jalbaab and gripping the rope that tethered her to the goat bleating softly beside her.

'Do you know what happened to my father?' she asked Keinan.

'Why? Do you?' he asked, quick, licking his lips.

'That's not an answer. Tell me. Please.'

Seeing the homeless woman with her children, Amina had had a sudden impulse to ask, a desire to know, no matter how bad the news was. But now, she wished she hadn't.

'I thought you might know because your father was behind it all,' she said.

'Oh.' Keinan's voice was devoid of boasting, or pride in his father. It was simply empty and tired.

'Never mind.'

'No,' he said. 'You have the right to know. I just don't want to be the one to tell you.'

She thought of Hooyo's dull eyes over the past couple of months, the anguish that allowed her to waste away, the fact that she never mentioned Aabbe or Roble. Hooyo must have already suspected that he'd been killed.

And now Amina did, too.

If Keinan didn't want to tell her, it meant the worst. Her father was gone. Forever. They had killed him. Was there anything more to say?

Fat tears rolled down her cheeks, a salty tang on her lips and tongue. She was glad it was dark and that Keinan was keeping a careful distance. She wouldn't betray herself with a single sniffle. She let the tears dry on her face. Her skin felt tight, like she was wearing a mask.

◆━━◆

They rattled the gate, Keinan shouting, 'Hello! Hello!' until they heard tottering footsteps coming their way.

'Who is it?' Amina recognised Rahmo's distinctive voice.

'It's Khadija Asad's daughter, Amina.'

'Amina! What are you doing here?' Rahmo was already fumbling at the gate and swinging it open.

'We need help, eeddo.'

Rahmo ushered them in, checking the road to see if anyone was following, then closing the gate and locking it. 'Roble?' she asked.

'This is Keinan, a neighbour,' Amina explained.

If she was surprised to see Amina with a young man who was not her brother, she didn't show it. 'What is wrong, daughter?' she asked.

'Hooyo's in labour,' Amina said. 'But it's not going well.'

The moonlight cast stark light on Rahmo's face, revealing deep creases in her cheeks, smile lines around her eyes. 'You better come inside,' she said. 'It will take me a minute to gather my things.'

They sat on wooden chairs, watching as Rahmo's mother gathered supplies from the kitchen cupboards and placed them in a large black bag. Rahmo disappeared then came back wearing different clothes. She grabbed the bag from her mother and started riffling through the contents.

Amina dialled Ayeeyo's number. 'We'll be home soon,' she said, when Ayeeyo answered.

Keinan followed Rahmo into the kitchen and whispered something to her, his face earnest, gesturing with his hands, as if emphasising what he was saying.

Rahmo nodded as Keinan spoke. She shook her head once or twice, the look on her face growing increasingly concerned. She heaved the bag across her shoulder and came into the kitchen. 'Amina, Keinan has told me that there are dangerous men looking for you,' she said.

Tears choked Amina's throat. 'Yes.'

Rahmo's gaze was compassionate. 'Perhaps you had better wait here,' she said.

'No, eeddo, Hooyo needs me.' Her voice cracked.

'Your mother needs to know you are safe while she's in labour,' she said, gently.

Amina nodded. 'All right.'

'Everything will work out, you'll see,' Keinan said.

She couldn't look at him. She wanted to believe he was right but it was impossible to know.

They stepped outside the door. 'Lock it when we're gone, Hooyo,' Rahmo told her mother.

Amina waited until they had left the yard and closed and locked the gate. She looked apologetically at Rahmo's mother. 'I'm sorry, but I have to go. My mother – she needs me.'

Rahmo's mother looked hesitant.

'Please don't try to keep me here,' Amina said. 'Please.'

Rahmo's mother nodded and followed Amina outside. She opened the gate. It clanged shut.

Rahmo and Keinan were still visible, moving swiftly down the street in the direction of her house. She stepped into the shadows and followed them, running lightly, swerving around potholes and chunks of footpath, skidding on gravel, falling down and tearing a hole in her jalbaab, then getting up again and running after them, always keeping them in sight.

She hadn't wanted to deceive them. But even if it meant walking right into the hands of the men who sought her, she couldn't wait here while Hooyo was in danger.

Chapter 13

Amina peeked through her front window into a crowded house.

An imam, Abdullahi Hassan and a third man – a stranger to Amina – stood uncomfortably in the front room along with Keinan and Ayeeyo. Abdullahi Hassan shifted his weight from one foot to the other. Keinan stood beside Ayeeyo, glaring at his father.

The imam pointed at the window and said something. Everybody turned to see Amina watching them. Ayeeyo closed her eyes.

Abdullahi Hassan stalked across the room towards the door. Amina leapt back and started to run down the steps just as Abdullahi Hassan flung the door open. 'Stop,' he commanded.

Amina stopped. She looked back. The man she didn't recognise flew down the steps and grabbed her arm, dragging her back up the steps and past Abdullahi Hassan. She stumbled and almost tripped, coming to a stop in front of the imam.

Although Hooyo's bedroom door was closed, they could hear every noise from inside. The uneasy silence in the front room was broken only by Rahmo's voice murmuring comforting words and Hooyo's occasional grunt.

'Amina, what are you doing here?' Keinan asked at the same moment Ayeeyo asked the men, 'What do you think you're doing? Let go of my granddaughter.'

'We're taking this girl into custody,' the imam said. He had a long beard and spoke out of the side of his mouth, his words slightly garbled.

'She's defacing public property,' Keinan's father said. 'She paints graffiti on the walls of buildings all around this neighbourhood, and the messages she paints are inciting people to revolt against the teachings of Islam.'

'What are you talking about?' Ayeeyo looked confused and angry. 'Not Amina. She's a good girl.'

'I love and respect Allah and the prophet Muhammad, peace be upon him,' Amina said. She spoke quietly, as she knew these men would want her to do. 'I would never do something that would incite people against Islam.'

'But that is exactly what you are doing,' the imam said. 'Just like your father before you.'

'My father was a good Muslim,' Amina said. 'Somebody's been lying to you.' She glanced at Abdullahi Hassan.

Twisting her arm, she freed herself from the man's grasp, then gasped as he yanked her back. She would have bruises where his fingers gripped her skin.

'What proof do you have that Amina is the artist you're looking for?' Keinan asked.

'Your father is the one who led us to her,' the imam said.

'Have you asked my father how he profits from this?' Keinan asked.

'Hush, son,' Abdullahi Hassan said.

Shame cracked Keinan's voice but he continued, dogged and steady. 'Members of al-Shabaab paid him to betray Amina's father. Do you think he's doing this for the good of Islam? Or is he doing it for the money? And if he's doing it for money, then is that how you determine the truth?'

The imam's face took on a resolute look, mirroring Keinan's. 'Abdullahi Hassan prays regularly at my mosque,' he said. 'If he says it's true, I believe him.'

'I also pray regularly at your mosque,' Keinan said. 'Don't you trust me?'

The stranger sneered. 'You've been blinded. Your association with this girl and her family has corrupted your good sense.'

'Wait,' Amina said. 'Please, let me show you something.'

The imam and the stranger looked doubtful.

'Please,' Amina said. 'I want to show you some of my pieces.'

She climbed the stairs to the second storey and brought back a cloth mosaic she had been working on and storing away from the family rooms so that she could keep it hidden. She had cut up strips of cloth into tiny pieces to create a large picture, a pattern creating a dark background with a white half-moon and the star of Islam.

'I am an artist,' she said. 'I admit that. I won't lie. And this is an example of the type of art I create. Is this a problem?' She looked at the imam for an answer. 'You would arrest me for creating this?'

He shook his head slowly. 'No, of course not.'

'So art itself is not a problem?' Ayeeyo asked.

'No,' he admitted. 'Islam has always had artists.'

'You were going to let these men take her and kill her, because she makes the flag of Islam?' Keinan asked, disbelief in his voice.

The imam furrowed his brow. He looked frustrated, a little angry – whether at one of the people in the room or at the situation, it was impossible to say. He opened his mouth but whatever he was about to say was interrupted by a piercing scream.

Amina dropped the mosaic and ran into her mother's bedroom.

Hooyo squatted on the ground, sweating profusely, her clothes pooling around her ankles. Rahmo held her hand, murmuring, 'Push, Khadija. You can do this. Push.' Hooyo looked up, startled to see Amina. Shaking her head, she muttered, 'As long as you're here, come and help me, daughter.'

Amina ran and knelt beside Hooyo.

'Put your hand on her back,' Rahmo instructed. She watched where Amina placed her hand. 'Lower. Lower.' She nodded when Amina was in the right spot. 'Now press hard.'

Amina pushed as Hooyo moaned. Hooyo guided her hand through the layers of cloth until Amina felt something spongy and wet. She yanked her hand back. 'What was that?'

'That's the baby's head,' Rahmo said.

Ayeeyo hurried into the room and noticed the baby's head crowning. 'She's almost here, Khadija! You can do it. Your baby is almost here!'

Suddenly, the baby seemed very real. Hooyo groaned and fell backwards onto the mat, unconscious for a few seconds. She opened her eyes, held her hands out – one to Ayeeyo, one to Rahmo – and stood, squatting down again, eyes closed.

'Would you like to catch the baby, Amina?' Rahmo asked.

Her heart beat rapidly but she crouched down, glancing back at the nurse for reassurance, putting her hands out like she was going to catch a ball. Hooyo groaned and strained and suddenly Amina was gripping something slippery like a fish, covered with a thin layer of white muck.

'Oh…' she cried, and clutched it close. 'Oh!'

Rahmo took the baby from Amina. 'It's a girl! You have a beautiful daughter, Khadija, just beautiful! A little flower!'

The baby was tiny, so tiny, and, underneath the layer of white stuff, her skin was greyish-blue. Amina looked away, afraid.

'Is she going to make it?' Hooyo propped herself up on her elbows to peer at the baby in Rahmo's arms.

Rahmo rubbed the baby's chest and belly, patted her bottom, and blew into her mouth until she started to bawl. Ayeeyo brought her a basin of warm water and she gently washed the baby until her skin was a beautiful nut brown. She brought her to the bed and gently laid her in Hooyo's arms.

'She'll be fine,' Rahmo said. 'And so will you.' Then she looked at Amina and burst out laughing. 'But your other daughter looks like she's about to faint. Amina, sit down before you fall over.'

Amina sat beside her mother. 'She's beautiful,' she whispered. And despite the baby's flat nose and funny, cone-shaped head, she was beautiful. Perfectly.

◆▸■◂◆

The front room was empty when Amina emerged a few minutes later. Ayeeyo had gone to the kitchen to boil water so she could clean the room and offer Rahmo a cup of tea.

She went into the yard, wondering where the imam, the stranger and Keinan and his father had gone. She had forgotten all about them during the birth and now she wondered if they would be back.

She found Keinan sitting on a rock near the fence. He was alone. He stood quickly as Amina approached, glancing anxiously at the house. 'Is everything all right?'

'My mother is fine,' she said. 'The baby is fine. But she's so little – little and brown, like a tiny nut.'

'I'm glad,' he said. 'I'm glad everything is fine.'

They stared at each other. Amina's heart pounded.

'Where did they go?' she asked, to fill the silence. 'Are they coming back?'

He shook his head. 'I think you shamed them.'

'Because of my Islamic flag?' *I should be more careful,* she thought. 'They might come back.'

'Maybe. But everything's changing in Mogadishu. Maybe they'll leave you alone.'

'I hope so.'

'I have a secret to tell you,' he said.

She waited.

He twisted the sleeve of his tunic, then kicked the rock gently with his foot. 'I've sold some of your artwork at Bakaara,' he said. 'The smaller pieces you made, like that mosaic.'

'What?' A rush of anger flowed through Amina. 'That was you? You took my work and sold it without asking me?'

'I didn't do it for me,' he said. 'I did it for you. For your father. For Roble. I saved all the money. I don't want a single shilling from the sales. I just need to fetch the money from my house and I'll bring it all to you.'

'Why didn't you tell me before?'

'I wanted to help you somehow but I didn't have a chance to tell you. You were so mad…'

Amina sighed. Her anger was already gone. He had meant it as a kindness. 'Thank you,' she said. Not everybody would understand why she wanted her work to be visible to all, and not kept for private use, but she had to at least try to explain this to Keinan. 'I don't do that work for money,' she said. 'I do it for the people of Somalia.

I want everybody to be able to see it. That's why I leave it where people will find it.'

'All right,' he said. 'But a little money never hurt anybody. It hasn't hurt me.' His jaunty grin was lopsided.

'I suppose,' she said. 'Well, I'd better get back to Hooyo and the baby.'

'Wait,' he said. 'Don't you agree? You think having a little money has hurt me?'

She smirked. 'I'll see you soon, Keinan.'

He shook his head. 'See you soon, Amina.' As she headed back into the house, he called after her, 'I could sell that flag of Islam you made. Get back to me about it, all right?'

She fluttered a hand in goodbye. She'd think about it. After all, they would need money in the coming months.

◆▬◆

After Rahmo left, Amina went back into the bedroom to see Hooyo. She was awake, holding the baby, wrapped tightly in an orange blanket, only her face poking out.

Amina knelt down by the mat. 'What's her name?'

'Didn't you have a name picked out for a little sister?'

'Jamilah.'

Hooyo smiled sleepily. 'Sounds just right to me.' She closed her eyes.

Amina touched Jamilah's soft, curly hair. She caressed the baby's ears – so little! – and touched her squishy nose, too big for her tiny face. Jamilah opened her eyes and stared up at her, unblinking. Her eyes moved left and right, left and right, alert for just a few seconds. Then she yawned.

'Hey, little flower,' Amina crooned.

Soon Jamilah and Hooyo were sleeping, little snores erupting from Hooyo's mouth, a tiny bubble forming on the baby's lips. The bubble got bigger then smaller with each breath Jamilah took, but it never popped.

Amina couldn't help giggling. She took a blanket and covered them. She'd never seen Hooyo look so exhausted – or so content. Time to leave her mother and baby sister to sleep in peace.

The scent of goat meat cooking with onions, potatoes and tomatoes drifted into the room. She tiptoed out and went to help Ayeeyo cook a very late dinner.

Chapter 14

Amina used a stick of charcoal to scratch a drawing of the map of Somalia on the wall of an abandoned shop near Bakaara Market. She drew the line of mountains to the north and created a curvy line, like ocean waves, for the sea. She drew an ocean liner and a Somali pirate ship lingering in the moonlit waters. She created the star from the Somalia flag above the ocean, and then a half-moon near the star, but not encircling it, in the way that symbolised the Islamic crescent.

Below her drawing, in big block letters, she wrote:

Peace for Somali Nomads, Wherever We Are.

It had been months since Aabbe was arrested, since al-Shabaab had kidnapped Roble and then been driven out of the city by African Union soldiers. So those nomads included the boys who had fought with al-Shabaab, some who were now returning to the city from various parts of the country where they had fought. Would the boys be able to go to school, find jobs, start businesses? And the girls, too, the ones who had served as wives to the soldiers? What would happen to them now? Would they be able to get an education, find husbands, have children? Would the people forget that they had been wives to al-Shabaab soldiers and let them live normal lives – or were their lives ruined? Amina hoped they would be welcomed back, as she would want to be welcomed back.

As the trickle of young men and women returned to their neighbourhoods, Amina couldn't prevent a desperate hope flooding her heart – that Roble would come back, too, one of these days. She didn't care if he was missing every limb on his body, which happened both to resisters and those who fought loyally for al-Shabaab. But it was impossible to say whether he would – or could – come back. She hoped for the best.

Keinan was busy these days. Despite the fallout with his father, which had been considerable, he still lived with his family. He had stopped going to school and had joined his father in opening a restaurant near Bakaara Market. They hoped tourists would soon return to Somalia.

He came by sometimes to see Amina and Hooyo and Ayeeyo. He would squat in the front room and play with Jamilah. Jamilah would coo at him and smile brightly, giggling at his loud voice and silly antics. Keinan was still Keinan.

Amina sometimes wondered what his visits meant, if their friendship would become something more than that. Certainly, Hooyo and Ayeeyo had come to see him as an extension of the family, a substitute son. Maybe they saw him as Amina's future husband. It was possible. Yet Amina wondered how she would fare with Abdullahi Hassan as a father-in-law. Mostly, she was too busy to think about it.

She had taken over Aabbe's studio as her own and nobody had argued with her. Now, she used his art supplies, including the blank canvases. She sometimes sold pieces at Bakaara Market, though now that Hooyo had gone back to her old job as a nurse at a private non-profit health clinic, there was less need for the money. The profits allowed her to buy new art supplies, when she wasn't making or finding her own, like she'd learned to do when she had no choice.

She had started creating a large collage with the odds and ends she'd been collecting on the street. A homage to Mogadishu, a tribute to the things they'd lost in the war. She planned to mount it high on their wall – where people could see it – now that she could practise openly as the Artist.

Life in Mogadishu was changing – slowly. The streets buzzed with the sounds of activity. Construction companies were hard at work making new buildings or restoring old ones. A shop and restaurant had popped up on the next street over. Vans and cars bearing the names of NGOs occasionally drove past the house, busy going here and there restoring the country. Amina's uncle in Norway was even talking about moving back to Somalia with his family.

It wasn't perfect. Squatters – and their goats – had

moved into the ruins of the post office down the street. Al-Shabaab had detonated a bomb recently, killing several and wounding others – all part of an attempt to destroy Mogadishu's fragile peace.

'That's to be expected,' Hooyo had said. 'Did you think we'd suddenly be a brand-new Somalia?'

But they were all grateful for the return to peace and a normal life. There was even talk of elections later that year.

Who knew what the future would bring?

◆▶■◀◆

'I think I'd like to become an architect,' Amina told Hooyo one day after school.

It was afternoon. Sunlight filtered into the front room and fell in dappled patterns across Jamilah's face. The alcove window cast a bluish hue over Ayeeyo, who was nodding off in the corner.

Hooyo's fingers gently caressed the baby's face and head. She had the look of a woman in love.

Even though the two of them still clashed, Amina had seen fleeting glimpses of that exact look when Hooyo looked at her, too. *Maybe,* Amina admitted to herself, *Hooyo loves me just as much as she always loved Roble.*

'Somalia needs good architects,' Hooyo agreed. 'That's a good career choice for an artist. A good career choice that will help our country rebuild.'

Amina kissed Jamilah on the head, traced two fingers across Hooyo's arm, and left. She had plans to work that day.

She had started to go further afield to find canvases for her work. Today, she found an unoccupied house missing doors and windows five or six blocks away. She wrote her latest poem on the walls facing the street, so that people would see it as they passed by.

She painted a large white square, then wrote in clear block print:

> In my box of memories, I will put
> a bag of Aabbe's paintbrushes,
> edges tipped in white and green and grey,
> like the ocean he was painting
> when they came and took him.
> I will put his warm brown eyes,
> a lock of my brother's curly hair,
> Ayeeyo's smile and even Hooyo's pretend grumpiness.
> I will put the breeze off the ocean, the swaying trees,
> bananas and spicy food.
> All the people I love, this country that I love,
> the maze of streets,
> the destroyed buildings.
> I will put all the good and some of the bad
> because even the bad is worth remembering.
> When this country is reborn,
> we will need
> all of our memories.
>
> A.

Author's note

I first encountered Somali refugees in Kenya in 1993, when I was working with street children in Nairobi during a summer break from college. Although the majority of the street children were native Kenyans, some of these children were Somali, having fled the violence in their countries with their families.

Working with street children in Kenya turned out to be life changing for me, as it redirected my interests toward the continent of Africa. I went on to receive two masters degrees in African history and now I focus much of my writing on the continent. Although my speciality is in southern Africa, during the course of writing *Amina* I found that Somali Africans are like Africans all over the continent: deeply hospitable. Many Somalis opened their homes and lives to me, despite the fact that I was a stranger. Their warmth, laughter, kindness and willingness to share their experiences both inside Somalia and now in the US touched my life in a way that I will never forget.

◆➤◆

Somalia endured a civil war from 1991 to 2012. During that time, the government made many attempts to create a stable, effective system for ruling the country, but failed.

This book is set in 2011, in the waning days of a militant rebel group's control of the city. In 2008, al-Shabaab, a fundamentalist Islamist group with ties to al-Qaeda, managed to take control of approximately a third of Mogadishu, the capital of Somalia. They ruled the city with brutality – banning music, games and women's bras, all of which they considered un-Islamic. People could be arrested for even talking about soccer.

Somalia experienced widespread famine in 2011, as the entire region suffered through a severe drought for the second year in a row. Hundreds of thousands of Somalis fled the country during the famine, made worse because al-Shabaab barred international aid organisations from delivering help in the regions it controlled.

A coalition of soldiers from around Africa, known as the African Union Mission in Somalia, began retaking Mogadishu in May 2011. When al-Shabaab abruptly quit the city in August 2011, fleeing south, war lords immediately began re-establishing themselves in the neighbourhoods that al-Shabaab had abandoned.

Despite this ongoing instability and the continuing problem of bombs and suicide attacks, Somalia experienced a real renaissance in 2012. In September 2012, with relative peace established across the country, academic and civic activist Hassan Sheikh Mohamud was elected president of Somalia in the country's first elections since 1967.

Al-Shabaab believed that art was haram for Muslims and they made creating art illegal during their rule over Mogadishu. During those years, artists either gave up their art or painted in secret. Many of them received death threats. Abdulkadir Yahya Ali, a prominent peace activist, founder of Mogadishu's Centre for Research and Dialogue and patron of the arts, was killed by suspected al-Shabaab soldiers in his own home. Since the return of stability and the ejection of al-Shabaab from the city (and much of the country), many of these artists have started to create art openly again. Mogadishu's Centre for Research and Dialogue, the centre that Ali created, has founded a project that displays paintings in public places in order to create dialogue about Somalia's past and its future. As of January 2013, they had mounted over twenty paintings in public places.

Timeline

○ **1960** Former Italian and British colonies in Somalia become the independent United Republic of Somalia.

○ **1969** Major General Mohamed Siad Barre stages coup, establishes Somali Democratic Republic and assumes presidency.

○ **1974–5** Severe drought causes widespread starvation.

○ **1977–8** Ethiopian–Somali War: Somalia invades the predominantly Somali-inhabited Ogaden region, seeking to incorporate the area into Greater Somalia.

○ **1980s** Opposition grows to Barre's military dictatorship due to government corruption, poor economic performance and persecution allegations. According to Human Rights Watch, thousands of Somalis killed, hundreds of thousands become refugees as militia groups rebel.

○ **1991** Somali Civil War: Barre's regime falls, rival clan militias capture Mogadishu. Civil war erupts with struggle between war lords

Mohamed Farah Aideed and Ali Mahdi
Mohamed. Collapse of central government.
Thousands of Somali civilians killed or
wounded. Somaliland declares independence.

1992–3 Estimated 350 000 Somalis die from
disease, starvation or civil war. United
Nations Operation in Somalia 'Operation
Restore Hope' led by United States (US)
airlifts food and supplies to Somalia.

1993 First Battle of Mogadishu: Between
US forces and Somali militia. Commonly
known as 'Black Hawk Down'.

1994 US troops withdraw. 20 000 United
Nations (UN) troops left behind to keep
peace and facilitate nation building.

1995 UN troops withdraw.

2004 Transitional Federal Government (TFG)
established. Islamic Courts Union assumes
control in southern part of the country,
imposing Sharia law. Fourteenth attempt
since 1991 to restore central government.

2006 Second Battle of Mogadishu: Al-Qaeda-
linked militants hold sway over much of city,
war rages with African Union troops. TFG
assisted by Ethiopian troops; African Union
Mission in Somalia and US military drive
out rival Islamic Courts Union.

2007 Battle of Ras Kamboni: TFG President and founder Abdullai Yusuf Ahmed enters Mogadishu and assumes presidency. Government relocates to Villa Somalia. First time since fall of the Barre regime that federal government controls most of the country.

2008 Militant Islamist rebel group al-Shabaab, with ties to al-Qaeda, continues insurgency against TFG, seizes control of key towns and ports, including approximately a third of Mogadishu. President Ahmed resigns.

2009 Al-Shabaab and militias force Ethiopian troops to retreat. Over 80% of south-central Somalia comes under control of Islamist insurgents. State of emergency declared as violence intensifies. Sheikh Sharif Sheikh Ahmad is installed as new president of TFG.

2011 African Union Mission in Somalia begins retaking Mogadishu. UN formally declares famine in southern Somalia as a result of worst drought in six decades. Millions of people on the verge of starvation. About 220 000 Somalis flee to Mogadishu and across borders to refugee camps in Kenya and Ethiopia. TFG, African Union Mission in Somalia and Kenyan army retake

Mogadishu from al-Shabaab militants, who retreat south. First airlift of UN aid in five years arrives in Mogadishu. US military starts operating drone attacks in Somalia.

2012 Federal Government of Somalia is established. Al-Shabaab loses Kismayo, their last urban stronghold. First elections held since 1967, with Hassan Sheikh Mohamud elected president. African Union Mission in Somalia troops remain in Mogadishu in an attempt to protect the still fragile peace.

2013 Rebuilding of Mogadishu despite sporadic bomb and gun battles in the city.

Glossary

aabbe father

adeer uncle; a polite way to address men who are your elders

alhamdulillah thank God

asalaam alaykum peace be upon you; the standard Muslim greeting

awoowe grandfather

ayeeyo grandmother

buraanbur traditional Somali dance performed by women at weddings

canjeero round flatbread; a food staple in Somali households

dhaagdheer mythical woman with excessively long ears who takes children at night and eats them

dugsi/duksi extracurricular school where kids learn to read, write and memorise the Quran

eeddo aunt; a polite way to address women who are your elders

Fajr first prayer Muslims offer between dawn and sunrise, as it begins to get light

halal permissible according to Islamic law

halwa sticky, jelly-like candy made of sugar, cornstarch and oil, and using nutmeg and cardamom for spice

haram forbidden by Islamic law

hooyo mother

imam Muslim religious leader

insha'Allah God willing

Isha   final, fifth prayer Muslims offer at night

jalbaab (s)/jalabeeb (pl)   long, loose outer garment that covers the entire body except the hands, face and hair

joodari   sleeping mat

keffiyeh   traditional Arab headdress worn by men

khat   mild drug; consumed by chewing the leaves and tops of the flowering plant *catha edulis*

khimar   preferred headscarf for Muslim women in Somalia

maraq   stew

maariin   word Somalis use to describe the rich, almost coffee-coloured skin unique to the Somali people

Maghrib   fourth daily prayer Muslims offer after sunset

muezzin   someone who calls the faithful to prayer five times daily from a mosque

Quran   holy book for Muslims

Ramadan   ninth month of the year in the Islamic calendar; during this month Muslims fast from dawn until sunset

Sharia   moral code and religious law of Islam

sijaayad   prayer mat

soor   corn meal mush

suhuur   meal that is eaten before sunrise during Ramadan

Sunnah   sayings and teachings of the Prophet Muhammad which prescribe the way of life – customs and norms – for Muslims

suras   chapters in the Quran

tasbih   Muslim prayer beads

wa 'alaykum asalaam   and peace be upon you as well; the standard response to 'Asalaam alaykum'

Find out more about...

Somalia and Mogadishu

Hamilton, Janice. *Somalia in Pictures,* Twenty-First
Century Books, Minneapolis, 2007

http://www.unicef.org/somalia

http://www.bbc.co.uk/news/world-africa-19112530

http://www.bbc.co.uk/news/world-africa-14094632

Somali youth

Hoffman, Mary. *The Colour of Home*, Phyllis Fogelman
Books, New York, 2002

Robert, Na'ima B. *From Somalia with Love*, Frances
Lincoln Children's Books, London, 2008

http://www.youtube.com/watch?v=R4yPAArtRN0

http://www.unicef.org/somalia/reallives_8480.html

Kafiya's story: http://www.unicef.org/
somalia/7734.html

Abderahman's story: http://www.unicef.org/
somalia/7847.html

http://www.unicef.org/somalia/reallives_11817.html

Street artists in Mogadishu

http://articles.latimes.com/2012/sep/19/world/
la-fg-somalia-artists-20120920

Child soldiers

Beah, Ishmael. *A Long Way Gone: Memoirs of a Boy Soldier*,
Sarah Crichton Books, New York, 2007

Acknowledgements

The Somali community of San Diego, California, welcomed me into their homes and lives with warmth, offering me thought-provoking conversations, delicious Somali food and friendship. In particular, I wish to thank Ahmed Farah, Abdisalam Farah, Rahmo Abdi, Fatuma Zahra Aideed, Lucky Farah, Nasteha Mohamed, Yasmin Farah and Mohammad Aidad.

I also wish to thank Andrew Bogrand from Refugee Transitions in San Jose, California, and Erika Berg and Ann El-Moslimany for connecting me to the Somali community in Seattle, Washington. I met with many Somalis in Seattle, including Hassan, Abdullahi, Abdillahi, Abdikadir, Anisa, Amran and others who may not wish to be named. Also in Seattle, Merna Hecht, Elizabeth Norville and Carrie Stradley helped to facilitate meetings with Somali teens, for which I am enormously grateful. Merna was also the inspiration for the poem beginning with the line, 'In my box of memories...' Thank you!

Mason Cornelius of Nova Midwifery helped with details about complications with Hooyo's pregnancy and possible herbal remedies.

Scholars and other writers who helped provide information or contacts include Keren Weitzburg, Richard Roberts and Abdi Latif Ega. Abdi answered many questions and, in particular, helped me to understand that while artistic practices in Somalia have changed as a result of Saudi influence, memories of Somali culture and artistic theories and practices would have survived the civil war.

For help with the finer points of Muslim thought, traditions and religious practice, I must gratefully thank both Ann El-Moslimany and Margari Aziza Hill. Both women quickly and thoughtfully answered questions ranging from 'Are beetles considered a halal food if a family is starving?' to 'As a Muslim woman, do you need pins to keep your headscarf on?' I am grateful for their patience. Any errors in the book regarding Muslim thought and practice, particularly in regards to Somali religious culture and practice, are all mine.

For reading drafts and/or discussing the book's plot, characters and related points: Siphiwe Ndlovu, Vaidehi Chitre, Emily Jiang, Matt Powers and Becky Powers. Special thanks to Abdillahi Muse for reading the final draft and marking up errors related to Somali culture and belief as well as daily life in Mogadishu.

While writing this book, I listened to a lot of Somalia's most prominent expatriate hip-hop artist, K'naan. I first heard K'naan before he was big, in Oakland in 2009, long before I became interested in Somalia. Thanks, K'naan, for your accessible, socially conscious hip-hop/reggae/dance-hall music.

Many thanks to my husband Chris, my parents (Becky and Dennis), and my mother-in-law Darlaine for watching Nesta while I worked. Thanks also to my team of babysitters and friends who helped out – Becky, Marci, Alex and Natty.

As always, I am grateful to my agent Jennifer Carlson, an extraordinary business partner and friend, and to the series creator and editor, Lyn White, and publisher at Allen & Unwin, Eva Mills.

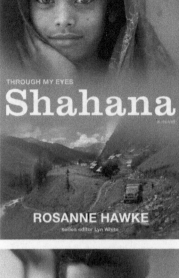
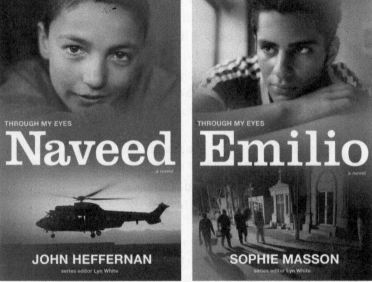